J   829.6308 BK

Fakih, Kimberly Olson

High on the hog

HIGH ON THE HOG

Also by Kimberly Olson Fakih

GRANDPA PUTTER AND GRANNY HOE

High on the Hog

Kimberly Olson Fakih

Farrar Straus Giroux

New York

J

Library of Congress Cataloging-in-Publication Data
Fakih, Kimberly Olson.
High on the hog / Kimberly Olson Fakih. — 1st ed.
p.   cm.
[1. Farm life—Fiction.   2. Family life—Fiction.
3. Grandparents—Fiction.   4. Moving, Household—Fiction.]
I. Title.
PZ7.F186Hi   1994   [Fic]—dc20   93-34214   CIP   AC

829. 6308

*To friends and colleagues
on Union Square and beyond*
MANHATTAN, MARCH 15, 1992

HIGH ON THE HOG

Meanwhile at the farm

Not for the first time, Trapp found herself staring at her great-grandfather's face, trying to measure the distance between the truth and what he was saying.

"If you can't smell it, it needs water," Great-Grandpa Hatfield said. He handed her a heavy garden hose and pointed her in the direction of the antique-looking outdoor faucet. "'Less it's winter. Nothing much stinks in winter. But spring and fall—pretty much everything stinks then. Growing or rotting, it all smells the same." His words faded as he ambled toward the front yard. "Just yell if you need me. I'll be under the oak—all you can smell there is summer."

It had been a dusty, sweaty June, and July didn't seem to be breaking new ground. The pig wallows that dotted the countryside, instead of stinking wetly, had to be hosed down daily so they wouldn't dry up and crack, without a scent. Dried up, they weren't much use to the hogs, whose interests on steamy days were confined to rolls in the cool mire and naps in the small outbuilding that housed them.

Trapp accepted the chore and wondered briefly if her parents, in a faraway place she didn't like thinking about, would appreciate the fact that she was watering dirt. She considered what they might be smelling just then. She liked the musty fragrance of city-size elevators—most of the ones in her part of the world were for grain, not people—but didn't take very well to the crowds in the hotel lobbies and restaurants she had visited with them. Small-town folk were supposed to feel that way about the big city that was routed more by congested elevators than by open freeways. She had often heard people beef, with something akin to pride in their knowledge of such things, about the slick, sealed-in scent of other people's oxygen, someone else's food, a stranger's reeking perfume.

Once, Trapp had been half-sold on the idea of city life. She had had good reasons for it—on visits to New York she loved the elegant hotels, flashy ice-cream parlors, people dressed up as if for a party. These days, the more she thought about it, the more the wallows seemed like a little piece of pig heaven.

When there was more mud than dirt, Trapp put the hose away and took refuge in the cool grass beneath the oak in the front yard. Next to her, Great-Grandpa Hatfield was curled halfway out of a battered wicker chair, leaning over a wooden bucket with an ice-cream paddle in it. One foot was propped on her baseball. He rolled it to her with the nudge of his shoe and kept on cranking.

Trapp looked for her mitt in the grass where she had left it. Great-Grandpa drew it out from behind him and tossed it to her. "Was afraid a bird would nest in it," he said.

The shade of branches overhead streaked and wobbled across the mitt. In the past month, her always winter-white legs had freckled only slightly from the sun's daily glare. Some afternoons were so sizzling hot that even grinding a baseball into her well-oiled mitt was too much of an effort.

Great-Grandpa had chopped up peaches to stir in with the cream, sugar, and eggs. As he turned the handle, water from the ice leaked through the staves of the bucket, making a dirty trickle amid the peach peels in a patch of dust. Drops of sweat ran off Great-Grandpa's brow and mingled with the mud.

He was old, Trapp knew. Her Nana Q, who had passed away last summer after the tornado season, had been old, and Great-Grandpa Hatfield was *her* father. Although much of the field work was handled by Rakes, the kit-and-caboodle caretaker, Great-Grandpa and Great-Grandma were still part of the running of the whole farm. It was the same land where Nana Q had grown up, where she, too, had probably watered pig wallows.

"Eustacia!" Great-Grandma Hatfield called from the front porch. "Eustacia, can you take some corn off the stalk for lunch?"

"Sure, Great-Grandma," Trapp answered, accustomed by now to her great-grandmother's use of her real name.

Eustacia was also Great-Grandma Hatfield's name. Everyone else called her Trapp, a joke left over from the days when she could shun her crib or any other enclosure without any help. "I'll be right back, Great-Grandpa," Trapp said, standing up.

"Now, lookee here, young lady," Great-Grandpa complained, intent on his task. "About this 'Great-Grandma' and 'Great-Grandpa' stuff you've been tossing around for the past month—or for years, I should say, with most everybody else—it makes us sound ancient, and ready for the mothballs. Let's you and me settle here and now on just 'Grandpa' and 'Grandma.' A little less of a mouthful, unless you aim to make me into one of our tuckered-out Forefathers."

"You do look a little like Thomas Jefferson, G— Grandpa," Trapp replied. "Only older. I mean, from the pictures I've seen in textbooks."

"Well, that's fine, that's fine," he mumbled, leaning back into the cushions.

"Soon as I get some corn shucked, I'll take a turn at the ice cream," Trapp said.

"Of course, they have electric doohickeys now," Grandpa commented. "A few years ago I would have said pooh on that kind of gadget, but I wouldn't mind plugging this old bucket in."

"You'll shuck, I'll crank," Trapp reassured him, and headed for the garden.

"Don't need electricity for shucking corn," he answered agreeably. He closed his eyes. A wisp of white hair fluttered over his wrinkled forehead.

The ears of corn were still compact and sweet-smelling on the stalk. Trapp had heard the expression "knee-high by the Fourth of July," but the corn had been much taller than that for the holiday.

By early August, the sky-high corn would be a hiding ground for farm kids playing games. Well into that month, most of the green corn—or sweet corn—would be brought in for eating and canning while the seed, or dent, corn continued to ripen. All the growers would plan their harvests, a time for calling in extra help, and sharing machines that could fell fifty acres a day. For now, the corn was in the milk, small and tight on the ear, with stalks only as tall as Trapp was. She could wade into the rows and peer along the tops, like standing in water up to her nose. Amid silky white tufts just beginning to peek out of each husk, she was part of an ocean of green—or at least a lake, bordered by trees that Grandpa Hatfield's grandparents had planted when they had settled the land.

The trees were still standing, long after the great-great-great-grandparents had passed away from this place. Maybe all those ranks and rows of yearly corn would be here when everyone else was gone, even her.

Trapp's head felt abuzz in the heat and haze. To clear her brain she focused on the huge painted wooden sign spelling "Boo!" that shone like neon in the sun. Rakes had made it; Grandpa pronounced it a "newfangled" scarecrow. Trapp preferred the other, more human-shaped warnings that cropped up here and there across the horizon. Rakes had stuffed several old gray business suits full of straw and devised briefcases that banged against the poles every time a particularly strong gust sailed past them. To Trapp one scarecrow was as silly as the other. But Grandpa was right when he said, "You wouldn't think so if you knew Rakes."

Rakes had his ways, anyone could see that, closer to those of a Native American than those of a sod-busting settler. He was as quietly passionate for what he called "nature's way" as he was about scarecrows and other man-made trinkets. "The sky's the limit to putting a scarecrow on a perch," he'd say. "They come in all shapes. And if it works, it's good enough."

The stalks waved and bobbed in the wind. Trapp didn't feel the breeze, but she could see it work across the corn tufts, the same way it had fluttered through Grandpa Hat-field's hair. She listened—Grandpa said he could hear the corn grow—but only a rustle of soft whispering leaves met her ears.

Grandpa was snoring softly into his shirt collar when Trapp returned to his side. She took her place in the grass to shuck the corn, yanking down the long green petals and working her fingers around the ear, then setting it free with a sigh. The husks flowed behind the ear like smoke from a rocket. She broke off the stem and put the ear next to her. Grandma Hatfield always picked off the last hairy strings in between the corn's teeth, so Trapp left them alone. She repeated the motion on several more ears of corn, then began to turn the crank of the ice-cream bucket.

The crank was almost too hard to turn. That meant

that the ice cream was finished. Trapp twisted off the lid, pulled the ladder out, and brought it to her mouth, ready to give the metal paddles a few quick licks.

"Eustacia!" Grandma called again from the porch. "Don't put your tongue on that cold metal! I'd have to cut it off!" Trapp shuddered. She hadn't known anyone was watching.

"And I'm ready for that corn," Grandma added. Yanking the rope to a large tarnished brass bell, posed just outside the porch's screen door, she sent a clanging into the air that would summon Rakes from the fields. The clamor startled Grandpa briefly before he settled back into his doze.

Trapp tossed the ladder on the grass, put the lid on the metal can, and, gathering up the corn, carried it and the ice cream awkwardly to the house. Her grandma took some of her load as Trapp approached, and together they slipped into the kitchen.

"The water is boiling—baby corn for lunch, just-picked lettuce, some pickles from the crock, and spoon bread," Grandma said. "And ice cream for dessert. That beats going to the grocery store, doesn't it?"

It was one of her great-grandmother's favorite subjects, and she never missed a chance to relate it: the value and bounty of farm life over the way of the new, or what she called—in general, addressing mostly Rakes because he agreed with her—"cellophane packages from slick salesmen with their polyester suits and huckster slogans."

Trapp personally loved grocery stores with their rows

of brightly colored cans and checkered walls of bottles and boxes. But corn on the cob for lunch and peach ice cream for dessert was hard to argue with.

"Trapp! Hey! I'm ready to shuck that corn!" Grandpa's voice drifted in through the screen door. She went to the porch and saw him sitting up straight. "Where'd you get to?" she heard him ask as he peered around.

"I'm here, Grandpa," Trapp called. "Lunch will be ready in a couple of minutes."

"Well then, I'd better get to that corn. If we save it for dinner, it will be too old off the stalk for your grandma," he admonished.

Joining her, her grandma put a soft, doughy arm around Trapp's thin shoulders and giggled. It was a high, girlish laugh, not at all the way she usually sounded. Trapp glanced at her face. She saw her great-grandmother watch the old man pushing himself up from the wicker chair, and in her eyes, just for a moment, appeared a soft, fond look, like the gaze Trapp had seen in brides' faces. She wiggled out of the elderly woman's hug.

"We'll wash up—you cook the corn," Trapp said over one shoulder, and ran toward the oak.

On city life
and country life and
somewhere in between, or when
farms no longer held livestock

N ow, this letter I got from your folks," Grandma
Hatfield said after lunch, leaning away from the
kitchen table and letting a page of thin paper rest
on her bosom, "says they found a place they like, but that
the paperwork hasn't gone through just yet, so they can't
arrange for the movers."

"Did they send a picture?" Grandpa asked. "Did they
say what it looks like, or how much land is around it?"

"Your mother says it's 'near private schools,'" answered
Grandma. "'Off Park Avenue with a large roof terrace
and small garden, in a neighborhood with lots of charm,
and very residential . . .'"

"That will mean no trees and short scrubby bushes,"
her grandpa interrupted. "And houses close together like
people on a bus, one looking just like another. Neat and
tidy, like."

He banged a fist down on the arm of his chair. "Hah! I bet it's attached to the houses on either side of it with no room for bluster in between! What's that they call them—'brownstones'? And no land around, that's for sure." He elbowed Rakes, who was quiet as usual, finishing his lunch. "No room worth a spit. What do you think?"

Rakes raised one glossy eyebrow and nodded. "Lots of people, though," he said mildly. "Maybe that's why they call the city the human frontier."

"Good one!" Grandpa said.

"Now, hush, Ralph," Grandma told him. "You don't know which end to milk when it comes to the big city. She calls it a town house, and that's probably how homes are supposed to be built there. It sounds nice, doesn't it, Eustacia?"

Trapp leaned her head on one hand, and twirled her spoon through the last of the peach ice cream. The cream was so fresh that it had left a milky film on her cold spoon. "I guess it sounds fine."

But it wasn't. Not at all.

Ever since April, when her father had announced that they were moving to New York City, Trapp had a feeling that nothing was fine, or ever would be fine again. A piece of granite seemed to have settled in her stomach, toward the small of her back, and it rocked every time she thought about the city, a new home, and a new school.

"If their plans go the way they hope, they're going to come here for a few days before the move," Grandma said. "Here, you read the letter yourself." She held it out to Trapp, who took it listlessly. Once again her great-grandmother had managed to say what was in the letter her own way before Trapp actually read it. That usually meant Grandma wanted to lighten the blow about something. Like her parents finding a house. To live in. Permanently.

"No land—not in the city," Grandpa repeated. Grandma gave him a bemused look and shook her head.

"It's true," Rakes joined in, putting down his spoon. "To a farmer the land is all, whether a big farm or just a patch of garden. No difference."

"But when you go east instead of going west and you wind your way around the bend from being a farmer to being a businessman," Grandpa said in one breath, "maybe you don't give a hoot about the land anymore."

"My great-uncle," Rakes said, turning toward Trapp, "used to tell a story."

"Now, hold it, Rakes," Grandpa interrupted. "Is this the uncle the kids called he-who-tickles-himself-and-makes-others-laugh?"

Rakes nodded.

"Go on, then," Grandpa said. "This'll be good." He was already grinning, but Trapp's brain felt too busy for her to be amused.

"When the gods created cities, they were all full up from drink and feasting—maybe even hung over," Rakes said. He stood and made his way toward the screen door before turning to look at Trapp. "And perhaps a little light in the head from all the belly-tossing."

Grandma sputtered, and Grandpa whooped. Trapp grinned, in spite of her worries. She didn't think the city was *that* bad. She just didn't want to live there. She didn't want to leave.

"Then what possessed them to create the countryside, I'd like to know?" Grandpa joined in, still laughing.

"Oh, he had plenty to say about that, too," Rakes said. "They were lying on their backs and staring at the open sky. Before they took a drink, while they were still bored and hungry, they created the great prairies and plains of the Midwest." Then he left.

"You all make it sound like New York is on another planet," Trapp said when he had gone.

"I hope you men haven't upset her," Grandma said. "All this nonsense about city and country. Why, home is where you make it, I always say."

"Sorry, Trapp, if an old man shoots his mouth off," Grandpa said. "What Rakes was saying—"

"It's okay," Trapp said. "It was a good story. May I be excused?"

"Run along," Grandma said. "I'll do the lunch dishes if you'll help me with supper."

"She always helps," Grandpa said. "You've been running her ragged since she got here."

Trapp liked that expression—but she didn't feel ragged. "I'll set the table before supper and wash the pots and pans after," she replied.

"Then what are you standing around here for?" her grandma said mock-sternly. "And I'm not running her ragged, Ralph. That bit of a girl has never looked healthier—all this clean air and fresh farm food."

The screen door slammed behind her, and Trapp

14

skipped off the front step. She was free again, free to ignore all her worries about the Move. She couldn't help constantly thinking about it; the least she could do was not have to talk about it. Not yet. Not until she had her heart straight. Not until her own plans were carried out.

Her younger sister, Maggie, was at camp for the summer, and didn't care *where* they lived. Her older brother, Sam, was, as usual, tagging along with her parents—she and Maggie called him Samsonite. He was changing from middle school to high school anyway, and seemed to believe that moving was only slightly more complicated than that.

Trapp held out; she alone was more than a little reluctant about the change of scenery. Life in Mason City, Iowa, suited her just fine. New York loomed like an alien landscape, frightening her. It was a place for tourists. It was not a place to live. For some reason, she had it in her mind that only grownups lived there. Home was here. Her insistence on that surprised *her* as much as everyone else.

She had told her parents about her reservations. That was why she was at the Hatfield farm.

"How about if I move in—just for the next few years or so—with Poppy?" she had asked. Poppy was the girl up the street who had never been more than a rainy-day friend, but her family had an extra bedroom and she was on the same school bus route.

"You're the limit, Trapp!" her mother cried when she'd heard the proposal.

"Well, why not?" Trapp asked. "It's better than moving away from here."

"But I couldn't up and leave you with the Joneses," her mother said. "Or any other neighbors. Or your cousins. Or the Hatfields. I couldn't leave you behind."

"The Hatfields—that would do," Trapp answered, but she had been half-joking back then. "I'd spend summers with you, and maybe when I'm in high school, I could move, too."

"But, honey," her mother replied, "not only are you making other people's homes a convenience for you—you know better than to treat neighbors like that—but families just don't divide up that way."

"Whenever I say things like 'everyone does it,' or 'no one does it,'" Trapp argued, "you tell me that every case is different. I want to live here, and you guys don't."

Trapp remembered that her mother had looked serious, as if she were honestly considering the request. For a moment, Trapp had begun to believe the idea was not going to be dismissed outright. Then she'd watched her mother's eyes fill with tears. "Honey, you know? Even just thinking about leaving you here"—her voice broke—"I just couldn't dream of it."

Trapp had appeared to give up the notion of staying behind. She had come up with other strategies, using all her powers of persuasion to convince them of the error of uprooting such a well-adjusted twelve-year-old. She found herself suddenly uttering words only grownups used—*persuasion, strategy, reflection, introspection*—and she began to talk to herself, just as she had seen people do on the streets of New York.

Trapp had worked hard to get her best grades ever, so her parents would see how happy she was in school. She had bombarded every weekend in May with temper tantrums. She had tried to get Maggie and Sam to revolt against the Move, without success. One day she almost went too far: she showed up at her father's office, thinking that she would talk his boss out of transferring him. Of course, she had turned chicken in the lobby, and found her way home. Later she'd discovered that her father no longer had a boss. Now he *was* the boss.

Her parents seemed to shift out of character for a while. Maybe they had come up with their own strategies to make her less resistant to the Move. If Trapp's artful efforts were rewarded at all, it was in the form of unexpected gentleness and extra attention from the whole family. Many of her favorite meals were cooked for supper, and of the three children, only she had not been asked to sort through her belongings and decide what to leave behind.

It looked like one big conspiracy. Maggie and Sam had, for some reason, shouldered her chores as well as their own, without any demands, and Trapp, feeling a little spoiled, had been left alone much of the time to watch television and read her favorite comic books after school and on Saturdays: *My Billboard Buddy*, about two runaways crossing the country in search of their mobile home after a change of heart; and *Odysseus, the Traveling Salesman*, which made her laugh, despite her moods.

In the lengthening spring evenings, when she took her bike out of the garage, no one ever tried to stop her from riding, or tell her it was time to go to bed, or remind her to wear reflective clothing. Every night, despite being allowed the run of the neighborhood, Trapp traveled only one path—up one hill, over an avenue, down another hill, and back toward home—as if to memorize each curve, streetlight, and house.

It was Trapp who had sealed her own fate at the farm. In early June, Trapp had been sitting on her mother and father's bed, helping her mother sort dozens of socks into pairs. Maggie had already left for camp, and the rest of them were soon to join Trapp's father in New York, in some furnished apartment he had rented over an antique shop, a bus ride away from Wall Street.

"We go to the farm almost every month," Trapp said.

"The same as I used to when I was a little girl," her mother added, a faraway note in her voice.

"We won't be able to do that if we live in New York."

"No," her mother said, sitting down next to the laundry basket. "We won't. We'll miss that. But there is bound to be something else we'll do that will mean just as much to us."

"Like what?" Trapp asked. What could ever mean as much as visiting the Hatfields?

"Well, we're looking for a house right in the middle of things," her mother answered. "But later on, when we've settled in, we'll still try to find a weekend cottage to visit as often as we can." Trapp saw her mother's eyes light up. "Maybe it will be a dump when we buy it—a dump on a piece of land—even near the ocean. We've always gone to Clear Lake when your father had time off. But an ocean—that might be far better. We'll fix that house from the bottom up, all of us, with our own hands, until it's ours. Wouldn't that help make up for the farm?"

Trapp shrugged. It wasn't just replacing one house with another, or a lake with the ocean. She couldn't say what it was. Like something brushing up against her in a dim light, every time she turned to face it, it was gone. A feeling she didn't have words for—not yet.

"Say," her mother said suddenly into Trapp's silence. "Would you like to spend some time at the farm this summer? I mean real time?" She stood up. "It's perfect. You'll love it. They'll love having you."

"What do you mean?" Trapp asked.

"While your father and I hunt for the right home, you can stay with the Hatfields. As soon as we move, you can join us and Sam. Oh, Trapp," her mother said, "won't it be ideal? You'll miss the farm more than anyone—it's only right that you go there."

"I—I would like to visit them," Trapp said, relieved. The thought of living in an apartment in a distant city was almost as scary as the move itself to a new house and new school. The farm would keep her away from that, for a while. After the rest of the family moved, well, she'd think about that later. "I'll go," she added, more strongly.

"Let me tell your father!" her mother cried. "Wonderful. I admit, I'm glad for them to have company this summer. This summer in particular," she said, trailing off as she groped for a matching sock. Trapp knew she was thinking of Nana Q.

"They're getting so old," her mother added softly. "If

you could help out a little, like you do around here, it will be easier for me to ask them to invite you."

"I'll help," Trapp said, thinking that her great-grandparents had always been old. Still, if she made herself useful at the farm, maybe she would never have to move. She would force her parents to see how necessary she was to the running of the place. "I like helping."

"Let's see," her mother said, already making plans. "You'd be there part of this month. Part of July. We'll get the house, and come get you."

Trapp was still at the farm.

She knew now that they wouldn't be coming until the end of summer or even later. Much as she loved the farm, it was hard to be so far away from her parents—a taste of what it would be like when she finally got her wish.

She couldn't picture where her family was. When they talked on the phone, she didn't know what chairs they were sitting in, or even what color phone they had. Sam sleeping on a sofa in a study her mother had described as tiny? Maggie at camp—she couldn't picture that either. None of them were in their right places. Even if they were together again, in New York, it still wouldn't be the same. Home was more. She knew it.

The temperature in the kitchen was already off the charts, and the parlor of relatives who didn't talk back or give bad advice to children didn't seem much cooler

D ays later, Trapp's great-grandmother moved through the front parlor with a cloth, rubbing the nonexistent dust off framed photographs and bud vases and heavy, dark-stained furniture. She hummed while she worked. Trapp, carrying the mop, watched the old woman polish the oval glass of each picture as she did every morning. They were brownish, faded photographs, of sober children lined up in stiff, high-necked clothing and grim-lipped adults with hollow cheeks and limned jaws, standing rigid as fence pickets. The ornate frames that embraced each picture marched in hoe-straight rows over the mantelpiece, along end tables, and across an oak ledge that perched behind the sofa.

Trapp didn't think of the people in the pictures as relatives. "Relatives" meant liveliness, commotion, and the more noise the merrier. Relatives came to birthday parties, and brought packages at Christmas, and baked casseroles in the oven for backyard potluck picnics. They came to school concerts and cheered good report cards. Their screen doors were never latched, and there was always room for one more at their dinner tables.

The people in the photos were more like "ancestors." She had come across the word in school, but it was as remote and peculiar on her tongue as the pictures were to her eyes—shadowy, still figures against pale surroundings that held no clue to their lives. Some stood in erect, schoolboy rows near tepees of shocked corn, gathered into clumps to shed rain. Others stood sternly outside the farmhouse she knew so well. But the trees in the photos were smaller, and there were details missing from the house, like the screened-in porch that Grandpa built before Trapp was born, so the scenes remained oddly unfamiliar to her. Even when Grandma pointed to the photos and told Trapp the names of the people, and who they looked like, and how they were connected to her, Trapp couldn't think of them as family relations. Their faces held secrets. Their poses and stares made her feel left out. She was excluded by their silence.

Peeking through the forest of solemn faces in many of the photographs was Rakes's serene face—actually, what looked like Rakes's face, but was the face of his father or maybe even his grandfather, men who were about the same age then as Rakes was right now.

He had been with them, Grandpa was fond to say, since the sugar maples in the lane had been mere seedlings amid bird droppings. "Oh, not *this* Rakes," Grandpa would say, stopping in the middle of one story or other about the farm and old days' bounty. "His daddy Rakes—or maybe his granddaddy Rakes, was it?"

For Trapp it was never quite clear where the women in Rakes's family had gone—surely he had a mother, at one point, and a grandmother as well—but the stories never touched on them. When Grandma had been pressed on the point, she had dismissed Trapp's questions as easily as blowing dust off glass. "It's the menfolk in that family that have the longevity built into their bones. And the stabilizers."

"Hand over that mop, honey, and get yourself outside," Grandma said to her now, interrupting Trapp's musings. "It's too nice a day for you to stay in this gloomy old corncrib."

"I love this room," Trapp said, not relinquishing her hold on the mop. She was sort of fond of the pictures, a remote attachment of the kind she held for some TV faces. But even those were more alive to her—they moved. "It's oldish," she added, as a compliment.

"I love it, too," Grandma said, picking up an oddball lamp without a bulb and wiping beneath its base. She set it down and straightened the shade. "I sure do. And I don't like to see these folks smudged," she said, pointing at the photos. "It's all they have to look forward to—a clean face and a shiny frame—in this cluttered haunt."

Trapp only half listened. She made a couple of jabs with the mop under a sofa. It sat high off the floor on ornate carved legs that swirled down from the arms. Embroidered pillows were tucked along the upholstered back, and

23

a fine tatted shawl was draped loosely across the cushions.

"Give me that mop, Eustacia," Grandma repeated more firmly. "Your heart's not in it today. If you want to be a help, let me look after the dust—I'll make sure it finds its way into the dustpan and not just into the corners."

Trapp decided not to insist on helping, in spite of her promise to her mother. Some days she worked so hard that she figured Grandpa and Grandma had forgotten what it was like before she came along. They would be in for a real surprise if she ever left.

"My, oh my," Grandpa would say to Grandma, "I don't remember how to shuck corn, it's been so long since I've done it."

Or her grandma, faced with doing a good number of dishes all by herself, would think it was high time Grandpa got her some help. "When Trapp was here, I got along fine without a dishwashing machine," she would have to admit. "But now it seems like there are more plates and glasses than ever."

It would be good to be missed, Trapp thought. She made her way out the kitchen door and onto the porch, where her baseball perched next to a nail where her mitt was hung. She slipped her hand into the cool leather interior and sighed.

Trapp didn't think anyone was missing her these days. It was as though she were floating, like a balloon, and everyone thought someone else was holding the string. For as long as she could remember, there had always been some force of gravity to keep her feet firmly on the ground, and a line that led directly home. Trapp felt sorry for herself and knew it; she believed for a few minutes that if she just drifted away, no one would really notice. Still, staying with the Hatfields was better than being anywhere else, especially when Trapp didn't know where anywhere else was.

The dew made dark wet stains on her sneakers, and the grass tickled her ankles. The *ke-shug, ke-shug* sound of Grandpa wheedling his lathe broke the stillness of the morning. For a minute she considered going into his shop to see what piece of furniture he was working on. The notion passed, and she turned away.

With all the gardening and housekeeping of the last few weeks, she hadn't had any real time to practice, and her pitching arm, though strengthened by the work, needed limbering up. Now was her chance, when Grandma had pushed her out of the house, and before Grandpa or even Rakes could find her and come up with something else for her to do.

She headed for the old barn.

T rapp rushed up the gravel path toward the barn, enjoying her sudden freedom. With only the rustle of the fields in her ears, she remembered a letter she was toting in her back pocket. Ever since it had arrived, she had read it in snatches, but now she sat down against the rough barn wood and tried to find out if her mother's enthusiasm was real, or, as usual, an all-out sales pitch to help Trapp ease into the Move. Like the letter her grandmother had received, it was mostly about the new house, but instead of the outward descriptions, this one was about the town house's interior.

"Your room," she read to herself, "is on a floor all by itself, with a staircase from the fourth floor that leads to your door and nowhere else. It's a dear, round room—a turret—with a domed ceiling. Actually, it has the shape of a silo. There, have I made you laugh? The current owner used it as a research room. The lawyers handling the sale asked if the owner would be able to rent the sweet garden apartment during the winters as a condition of the deal, and we've of course agreed. There's plenty of space for her.

"I've got wallpaper samples ready to send you, if all goes through. Oh, Trapp, we're all going to be happy here; I do hope you think so, too."

Just like her mother, Trapp thought, to write exactly the way she talked.

She refolded the letter.

If she went along with her parents' plans, she was to be stuck away from the rest of the family in this new home.

No, that was unfair. After years of sharing a room with Maggie, any room by herself should have sounded perfect. If the house was theirs. And if she liked the wallpaper that her mother had already picked out. If. If. No. No.

"I will not go," she muttered. She realized she was talking to herself again, shaking her head.

Scooping up her baseball gear, she strode away from the barn before turning around for her windup. It would be hours before the mail came, and there wouldn't be another letter so soon from her parents. Even if there was, she wasn't sure she would want to read it. Letters made her feel more detached, as if her family's lives weren't part of her own.

What did her mother expect—that picking out wallpaper was going to make her warm to the idea of moving, when nothing else had?

Trapp angrily aimed the ball at the side of the barn and snatched it out of the air when it bounced back toward her. She liked the sound of the ball hitting the smooth leather of her glove with such force. Again and again she slammed the ball into the wall. Her motions became rhythmic and fluid. Slam and catch, slam and catch. Her arm ached from the exercise. But the pain didn't matter; it subsided as she repeated each precise movement, savoring the moment of release as she pitched, and relishing the smack of the ball back into her glove. Slam and catch, slam and catch, and then just a slam, and crack! And quiet—no ball came zinging back.

Trapp's concentration was broken.

It took her several moments to register that this time the ball had gone through the old barn wall.

Trapp ran up to the broken board and peeked in. She couldn't see her ball in the thick piles of straw that covered the floor. She wasn't sure if she was in trouble or not. It was the first time in her whole life that she had broken into something so big—it made her mouth dry that she thought of it that way. Not just breaking something; she'd done plenty of that. But breaking *into* it.

Maybe the wall had been rotten already. Maybe it had just been barely hanging there, waiting for someone like her to give it a push.

Maybe, as her great-grandfather liked to say, that board was as solid as the day it was pinched from a tree.

Entering the barn, and in spite of her worry, she grinned at the sight of many polished pieces sitting at different angles in the straw. They had not been placed randomly; Grandpa Hatfield knew where the leaks in the roof were, and each piece of furniture rested where it wouldn't get wet. It looked as if everyone had left a gathering suddenly, without putting anything back in its proper place.

Neighbors brought Grandpa Hatfield their broken chairs or legless tables, and he made them new again. He could do simple repairs, or recarve a fourth leg to match the other three, no matter how intricate the work. Some people wanted the furniture back. But usually they dumped off broken and battered pieces and told Grandpa to fix them or toss them, whichever he chose. And Grandpa never wavered; he always fixed them. Even Trapp knew it was a point of pride with him. "Well," he'd say teasingly, "there're these voices that keep after me, nagging at me and telling me what to do. I just can't get myself to disappoint them." Trapp assumed he was saying something funny, and didn't mind not knowing exactly what he meant.

Each summer, a Salvation Army truck pulled in, was loaded up, and carted off the pieces. But until then Grandpa Hatfield stored the furniture in the otherwise empty barn.

Trapp walked among the various pieces, looking for her ball.

She was in the center of a marvelous distraction. A pleasant one. The need to find the ball waned a little. It could wait.

In one corner of the barn was a pyramid-shaped stack of mason jars, flooded with light beaming through a nearby window, and sparkling in the midst of dust and hay pollen.

Cobwebs softened the corners of the barn, draping over still-sturdy rafters. An American Rotary plow was placed next to a fireplace popcorn popper, all bent and rusty. Other old farm tools marched like musical notes up and down the barn walls.

Trapp knew she had seen no photographs of the inside of the barn in her great-grandmother's collection. Its exterior, like those of other buildings on the farm, loomed in the backgrounds of many pictures, with people gathered in step-and-stair posed group shots. Grandma had said there wasn't enough light inside; that the itinerant photographers that crossed the rolling prairies had to work outdoors.

It was hard to think of the flat folk who lined every surface of Grandma's polished parlor as breathing, sweaty, flesh-and-blood men, women, and children who would have paid this barn a call twice a day just for normal chores alone.

Trapp tossed her mitt aside.

With her pointer fingers, she pulled her eyes into two long slits, blurring her vision. It was a trick she used to make the pictures on the television screen look clear when the reception was bad. All the while, she tried to hear the voices of others in the barn, and feel the steamy, moist presence of livestock, and see the people and older children from the photos bent over their work.

She almost thought she glimpsed them. Herself included: just one more count in the bustling, sighing scene.

The restored furniture shimmied back into focus, blocking out her imaginings of the way it used to be. Trapp let go of her eyes. She was alone, with a warehouse of furniture and the smell of newly applied beeswax and very old straw.

Restlessly she tried out a few chairs, but none were padded or upholstered. Sitting down gave her a different perspective on the barnscape.

And there, next to a shiny oak desk a few paces away, was her baseball.

Trapp rounded up her mitt and set it down next to the ball, which looked no worse for its trip. The desk's center drawer was crooked, tilting in on one side. She gave the drawer a hesitant yank, trying to bring it flush to the opening. But it was stuck.

Tugging harder, she bent over until her eyes were level with the darn piece. With one last, irreverent tug, she put all her weight into separating drawer from desk. It still wouldn't budge.

The crawl space under the desk was just her size. She sank to her knees, prayer-like, feeling the scratchy hay against her bare legs like hair pants. Pulling herself determinedly under the desk, she raised her eyes to the space where the drawer was. One peek told her that it was wedged in, off its rails from the force of her pitch. For a moment's lapse, fleeting as the flapping of a mockingbird's wing, she had a shivery feeling of pride about that pitch. Jeez. All the way *through* the wall and it still had enough impact to jam something. Even Sam would be impressed.

Her boasting quickly dwindled. She might have damaged a piece of furniture that her grandpa had carefully restored. She worked her thin fingers up into the space over her head, trying to grasp the drawer and force it straight.

Finally the drawer eased a bit. Suddenly it was free.

She climbed out, pulled the drawer all the way toward her, checking to see if the runners had been damaged, and turned it over in her hands. It wasn't heavy, because it was not very large, and other than a small splintered place, it looked as good as new.

Her fingers felt another rough spot. She twisted the drawer around. Carved in the back, on the outside, where it would be hidden from view, even to the person who used the drawer for storage, were the initials "RH + GS." She saw the word "forever," in quotes, next to the initials, the "o" and "e's" more square than round, declaring the less-than-professional skills of the carver.

"RH"—that was probably Ralph Hatfield, her grandpa. And her grandma's maiden name was Shelton, the second part of "GS." But the "G"? Grandma was Eustacia. Trapp dropped down into the straw, thinking while she scraped at the carving with her fingernail. The "GS" person was probably the one who had delivered the desk. Grandpa would have seen the initials when he was working on it. All she had to do was ask.

Even asking bothered her. Her great-grandparents had been married for more than six decades. Their sixtieth anniversary party had taken place the summer she was ten. She remembered the large, buttery roses that decorated the cake; she and some bratty cousins of hers had fought over them—and were all sickened by their penetrating sweetness.

Never in her lifetime had she thought of her great-grandparents as anything but a whole—a unit; or perhaps like her left and right hands clasped together, matching; or her two feet; or the two legs of a pair of jeans. Did "forever" mean love? And wasn't forever sixty years or more?

Could someone be married to someone else and, secretly, love someone he had known as a young man . . . ?

Trapp's head felt murky, hot, and hazy with question marks. What if the initials had been carved recently? She turned the drawer over in her hands. No. These were old. Dirty and smudged.

All she knew about what others called romance was what she saw on television—people Sam's age and older going on dates, and kissing in cars. An alarming, graphic picture of her great-grandfather as a teenager came to her. His elderly head sat on top of her brother Sam's body, which was clothed in sweaters and jeans and walked with a youthful step, in lavish, springy sneakers.

He was strolling with a young girl. But because Trapp didn't know who GS was, she couldn't put a head on top of the teenage girl, dressed in a sassy skirt and baggy sweater. It seemed crude, as if her grandpa were parading around with someone her own age. It mixed her up, like the goofball collages her sister Maggie made.

Trapp put down the drawer and picked up her glove. It smelled familiar; she plunked the ball into the hand-shaped pocket. The two pieces fit together perfectly.

Grasping them to her chest, Trapp remembered pictures of her grandpa with his parents, a stranger in pressed clothing and with arched, wavy hair, gleaming with some sort of tonic. Only his eyes had looked familiar to her. It was like those pictures of ancestors; only he, a relative, was blending in. She wasn't sure, suddenly, whether Grandpa was an ancestor or a relative. Did he know GS then? Was she someone who wished for him to come around to her house to visit, dressed up for Sunday, and smiling so confidently?

Trapp's heart twinged inside her ribs, thinking about her grandma waiting to go on a date with her grandpa. But he was so busy with GS that he never showed up. Had her grandma ironed a long, old-fashioned dress and made her hair shiny and found a big bow to tie on her braid? And then waited? For nothing?

Tears fell on Trapp's mitt and stained it. The stitches on her baseball disappeared from view, and she forced herself not to cry more. A deep breath helped her feel silly.

"Eustacia! Honey, come on in!" she heard her grandma call. It was a voice from a different time and a different country. It brought her back. She felt her sneakers on her feet, real and firm upon the barn floor.

"Coming," she yelled. Carefully she fed the drawer

back into its spot. It was simple. She would ask her grandpa about GS. She would find out if "forever" really meant—well, just that. With his answers, maybe she would know if she would exist, the way she was, if he had married GS and started his family with *her* instead of with Eustacia Shelton, the only woman Trapp could ever imagine being her great-grandmother.

More mealtime conversation than you can shake a stick at, and a chance for some chowchow and a new friend

I'll have Rakes take a look at the hogs," Grandpa said at lunch, "and ask around in town about prices. Haven't had to sell livestock in a long time." Trapp couldn't tell if his tone was sad or composed. "Don't know what a good hog will fetch these days, but I won't mind letting those wallows dry up." Looking up at Grandma and Trapp, he asked, "Where is Rakes? Doesn't he need food in his gullet anymore?"

"I fixed him a box lunch," Grandma replied. "He said he'd be outdoors all day. He said he was going over to Ring Road."

"All right, then, that's just fine," Grandpa Hatfield answered, picking up the jar near his plate.

"Corn's the kind of dish you don't know whether to put sugar on or salt," he said, spooning out some chowchow. "Say, young lady," he continued, addressing Trapp.

"Do you think you might like to meet the local entertainment around here—maybe make a new friend?"

"No, Grandpa, I do not," Trapp answered. The words sounded less like a joke and more like she meant to be smart. Too late. She saw Grandpa's eyes flicker as he looked back at his chowchow. He had been watching her with curiosity, but now dipped into the jar again.

The corn relish was flecked with red pimiento, finely chopped carrot, bits of green pepper, parsley, and lemony coriander seeds. They had it with anything they ate, lunch or supper. In July and August they always used less of it, just to make sure the supply lasted till the next season's batch was put up.

"What I mean," Trapp added, "is that I'm really happy just being here. With both of you. And I guess, with the move and—oh, I'll have to make friends soon enough. That's all I meant."

Grandma coughed mildly. "Ralph, I can think of another person who didn't need any company but his own, traipsing around the farm all day long." She beamed at Trapp. "That's right, isn't it, Eustacia?"

"Yes, Grandma," Trapp replied. She felt like a creep. She was certain she had hurt her great-grandfather's feelings. "Listen, Grandpa, why don't you go ahead and tell me who you mean?"

"You sure?" he said, his eyes lively again. "Well, as many times as you've been here, I don't think you've ever met the Stuttgards—that'd be Don and Gabby—who have the land out by the highway."

Trapp shook her head. People named Don and Gabby

didn't sound like the "local entertainment" to her. She waited for her grandfather to go on.

"Don's grandson—great-grandson?—can't think of his moniker just off the top, hold it—well, anyway," he said, "he's been living with them the last few years—with Don, that is, because Gabby's not around all the time—and he's just your age. He's been a bit of a tumbleweed—his folks move around a lot—but he's made Don's place his homestead. He's settled down real nice, but otherwise he's a genuine live wire," Grandpa added. "There should be a lull in the work for a couple of weeks—we've detasseled, sprayed, weeded, and every other darn thing—so I'm sure Don can spare him."

"If you'd like to meet him, just say so," Grandma said. "We'll have him over. It would be nice to do the Stuttgards a turn."

Trapp saw the rest of her summer laid out in front of her like a Monopoly board: it would be a combination of working the farm and entertaining some lonely boy as a reprieve from detasseling in the name of good-neighborly behavior. She wasn't sure—would it make time go fast or slow? She missed her parents, but if fall was a long way off, so was New York, and her confrontation with them. She still had told no one that she didn't plan to go; she could hardly believe she would get away with it. So did she want summer to slide by, or to linger forever?

Forever. That word again. She had intended to ask her grandpa about it.

Grandma was still talking. "That's just screwball. I can't remember his name either," she told her husband.

"Who is Gabby?" Trapp said suddenly. To herself she was thinking: Gabby Stuttgard? GS? But then she remembered that Gabby's name would have been different sixty-odd years ago. She would have been a GS only when she married. "Is Gabby his wife?" she persisted.

Her grandparents glanced at her and then at each other. They broke into broad grins. "Not unless it's now legal for brothers and sisters to marry each other," Grandpa told her.

"Ralph! Hush!" Grandma said, shaking her head before mending her smile. "No, Eustacia. Gabby lives out East. She's only back summers. As for Don's wife, well, she died a long while back."

GS? Trapp thought. Is that you? She would definitely let the grandson come for a visit. She might find out a lot from him. "But what about Gabby's husband?" Trapp asked. "Did he move in with them, too?"

"Gabby Stuttgard? Married?" Grandma said, smiling again. "No, she never did. Some scamp broke her heart —oh, a hundred years ago—and she never recovered. Never married."

Trapp looked quickly at Grandpa Hatfield. He was chewing chowchow as if his teeth were his own. He shrugged at her, his mouth full.

"Fine," she said, intrigued. "I'll meet this boy. What did you say his name was?"

Grandpa took one last swallow. "Something like . . . a city," he answered. Grandma shook her head and tapped her forehead, trying to summon her memory.

"A city," Trapp repeated. "Like his name could be

something like Minneapolis, or Sioux Falls—or Ames, Iowa?"

"Or Cedar Rapids," Grandpa said, teasing her.

"Cleveland!" Grandma said suddenly. "His name is Cleveland."

"That's it!" Grandpa joined in with a shout. "But I've heard he wants to change it."

"I should think so," Grandma told him. "Something simple."

"To what?" Trapp asked.

"Chattanooga," Grandpa said with a straight face. "As in Tennessee."

Wherein the beans
and the Stuttgards come
on kind of sudden, and local
entertainment substitutes for
Saturday morning cartoons

Trapp was bent over the bean patch, mornings later, trying to remember if Grandma had told her to pick the beans that had already dried off in the sun or the ones with dew on them, still in the shade part of the kitchen garden. The poplars, like fingers pointing to the sky, made long shadows over the fields.

She turned toward the sound of a truck. It jerked and wavered along the horizon, its wheels barely touching the ground. If Trapp hadn't known better, she would have thought from the way a small person was bouncing around in the back that the truck bed was made out of trampoline material rather than hard, cool metal. That instantly brought to her mind Saturday morning cartoons. The boy, for it was a boy, flopped first on his stomach and then on his back, yelping each time like a puppy being

41

rough-scruff-handled by its mother, as the truck turned down the lane of sugar maples.

With one last heave, the truck bumped over a rut in the road and came to an abrupt, shuddering stop. With a huge guffaw of the springs beneath the cargo area, the boy, with bony legs and plaid shorts, was catapulted over the side. Trapp wasn't sure, but it appeared that he did a somersault before landing with a thump on his backside in the dirt, looking as if his lungs were in a state of collapse. He grumpily got to his feet and brushed his shorts off.

"You think you could get those shocks checked, Don?" the boy called out between breaths. Trapp knew that he had seen her, and that he realized she had witnessed his fall. She smiled, only half-embarrassed for him. Mostly, he had looked comical, like a colorful mass of contortions, shapes, and rough edges flying through the air, unhindered by gravity.

Although she knew the man and woman who emerged from the front of the truck to be the expected Stuttgards, Trapp was immediately reminded of Jack Sprat and his wife—only reversed. Don was round as a pinball wearing a hat, in worn overalls that emphasized his shape. His face was a bit more weathered than his clothes, and his teeth were straight and white in a tan, smiling face.

Gabby was tall, and thin as a stalk of corn, with short, boyish white hair—a pluck of tassels and silks—around a long, lean, bespectacled face. In narrow jeans and a shrunken, cropped sweatshirt, she looked wizened but wiry for an elderly great-aunt.

That meant the boy was the famed Cleveland, who had already provided some local entertainment.

"Well, boy, you do know how to make an entrance," Don said, chuckling as he slammed the truck door. "This must be Trapp in the vegetable patch," he added, rolling toward her with one hand outstretched. Only a limp in his gait reminded her that he was an old man. "I'm Don Stuttgard. And I'm going to make that Ralph an offer for his hogs," he added, waving in the direction of the wallows.

"Hi," Trapp answered. She took Don's dry hand, which wrapped her own warmly.

"I'm Gabby," the woman said as she and Cleveland approached. She didn't offer her hand.

Gabby stood tall and straight over Trapp's head, a towering figure like the Jolly Green Giant that joined earth and sky. She moved closer and looked at Trapp with friendly brown eyes behind small, plain round glasses, her shoulders slightly stooped, with both hands in her pockets. "And this is Cleveland." She continued to gaze at Trapp with interest.

Cleveland nodded in Trapp's direction, but didn't have a chance to say anything. Her great-grandparents burst through the screen door, pouring out of the house with the "Hallooos" that preceded them, the way they always did when company arrived. Trapp was beginning to wonder if the beans were feeling crowded.

Grandpa hugged Gabby, Trapp noticed, and so did her grandma, who also wrapped her arms around as much of Don as she could reach.

"Good to see you, Gabby," Grandpa said gruffly. Trapp saw he was shorter than Gabby; she saw, too, that neither of the Stuttgards seemed as elderly as the Hatfields, even though Cleveland looked her own age.

Her grandpa put out his hand for Cleveland. "And here's old Cincinnati!"

"Cincinnati," Cleveland repeated quietly after him, unprotesting.

"Coffee's on the stove," said Grandma.

"Let's go in where we belong and rest our feet," Grandpa added, "and leave the outdoors for the young ones. Nice to see you," he said to Cleveland as Grandma pulled him out of the bean patch. Cleveland and Trapp were left standing there while the adults ushered themselves toward the house.

" 'Give it a rest . . .' " Trapp started to mumble.

The boy looked right at her and added, " 'Old Alpine's the Best.' The new prairie billboard out by the highway. Exit 7."

"That's the one," said Trapp, staring at the ground, pleased.

"Well, looks like we better get these beans picked," Cleveland said, "while the sun dries off the dewy ones."

That's it, Trapp told herself, reaching for a bean. "Leave the dewy ones on the vine. Pick the dry ones in the sun. Thanks," she said, turning toward him. "Do your—they, Don and Gabby—grow them?"

"Yes, they do," he replied. "But I'm not normally so closely affiliated with such intricacies of the harvest—I mean, old Don won't let me pick much, because I tend to pull up the entire plant."

"Oh," Trapp said. He had spun such a nice long answer from such a simple task.

"But this morning Gabby said the beans had come on kind of sudden, and we all had to pitch in," he continued. "Therefore, everything I know about beans I learned this morning."

"Oh," Trapp said again.

"So never let it be said," Cleveland added, "that I don't know beans."

If she had known him better, she would have groaned at the joke. Instead, Trapp just smiled dutifully and went back to her task. He bent over to help.

"By the way," Cleveland said, unfazed by her silence, "I'd appreciate it if you'd call me Cleaver—it's a name I'm trying out this summer."

"Why?" Trapp asked, running her fingers through the half-filled bucket of beans.

"Don't you think it sounds unusual—mysterious and sort of violent?"

"I think," Trapp said slowly, "that if you want an unusual name, you've probably got it."

"What's Trapp short for?" he asked, raising his eyebrows the way Grandpa Hatfield had earlier.

She grinned and ducked her head, and then was suddenly sad, remembering how often she would have to answer that question in a new city if her plan didn't work. This time, though, she didn't have to answer. Grandma

Hatfield did it for her, as usual, promptly, like the ringing of a bell.

"Eustacia!" she called from the kitchen window. "You and the boy come in for some muffins."

"Okay, Grandma," Trapp called back. She turned to face Cleveland, waiting for him to make a joke about *her* name. He looked worried.

"I can call you Trapp, can't I?" he asked anxiously.

"Yes," she said, staring at the damp beans still on the vines. They were done picking for the day.

"Good," he said. "Eustacia's a nice name, but maybe if I call you Trapp, you'll call me Cleaver."

She nodded, but did not answer. For some reason, Trapp didn't feel the need to answer, to spell things out for this boy. She picked up the bucket and her mitt while Cleaver watched. He nodded agreeably, and followed her into the house.

On bonding, or why corn-fed folk of the Midwest are so likely to get on together

L et's go to the barn," Cleaver said when they were both stuffed full of muffins. The adults had taken their coffee out to the front porch. "Let's see all that furniture. Last time I was here, your great-grandpa only had a few pieces. This time I want to see everything."

He was leaping around Trapp in circles, reminding her again of a small, yapping puppy, only this time nosing around a monarch butterfly. She wondered if he was always so excitable and talkative. Also like a puppy's were his too-large feet, in black high-top sneakers, and too-large hands, which he used at all times in gestures that accompanied his words. His body was thin, in his dark shorts and white T-shirt, and his black socks made his bony legs look even storkier. But his leaps were springy and compactly elegant, and when he walked, he seemed to glide forward in space, as if on wheels.

She wasn't sure she wanted to return to the barn. The desk was a kind of a secret to her. But she wanted to show the hole she'd made in the wall to *someone*. It might be pretty impressive to Cleaver. She didn't have to mention the desk—or the initials. Not till she figured it out. Or at least not till she knew him better.

Still, Trapp felt an instant kinship with this boy. Maybe it was because he was living with older relatives just as she was—or hoped to be. If Sam or Maggie had been jumping around her, teasing her or pestering her with words, she would have begged to be left alone. Instead, with Cleaver, she silently opened the screen door and let him hop down the kitchen steps. "We can go to the barn," she agreed quietly.

Looking out over the green fences of corn as they walked, Cleaver said, "I've always wondered—aren't your great-grandparents old to be farming so much of the land? I mean, Don's old, but he has lots of help. Even that kitchen garden looks big, considering how ancient your great-grandmother is."

Trapp thought about telling him it was none of his business, but then realized with a jolt that she forgot, sometimes, just how old her great-grandparents were— more than eighty years old each. And eighty was up there near a hundred, as far as she could tell.

It was a reasonable question, she decided.

"They are old," she admitted. "But there's Rakes. And a neighbor—Don and Gabby probably know him—rents the part of Grandpa's land that's next to his own. I think he and his sons help with the plowing in the spring. They share the highboys and combines, I know."

"These old farms," Cleaver said, "aren't going to be around much longer." He balanced on one leg and leaned over to pluck a sprig of clover from the gravel path where it had sprung up.

"What do you mean?" Trapp asked, stopping suddenly. They had walked to high land. Rustling fields of corn stretched out in all directions before them. The farm had always been part of the landscape, as long as she could remember. The ancestral photos proved it, with the outbuildings always in the background.

"Don says that all the little farms are becoming part of one big farm," Cleaver answered, facing her. "When your great-grandpa dies, that neighbor you mention will probably just buy this farm outright."

"No," Trapp said loudly. Then she lowered her voice. "Grandpa told me the whole country is one big farm that no one person can own." Unexpectedly, her mouth felt clenched tight with anger and sadness, but she had to speak. "He's old, but he's strong. It will be years before he—you know." Cleaver was awful, she thought, talking about Grandpa Hatfield like that.

"I'm sorry," he said quickly, almost before she finished her sentence. "I was just talking, and I didn't think about what I was saying."

Her throat still closed and thick with dread and fury, Trapp considered her family's Move in the fall. Not everyone moved. Not everyone left the homes they had lived in for what seemed like forever. The farm—her great-grandparents' farm—would always be there. Nothing her family did could get them away from that.

Cleaver still peered at her hopefully. "Don says I do that all the time," he told her. "I really am sorry, Trapp."

"It's okay," she said, and meant it, because he did.

He nodded gratefully, and fell back into stride with her as they took the last few steps to the barn.

Cleaver saw the hole almost immediately.

Maybe he'd seen her looking at it, waiting to see if he would comment. Maybe it was as large and gaping as she had thought it was.

He ran up to the hole and put his hand to the splintered boards and the exposed, raw wood.

"What caused this?" he asked. "A meteor?"

Trapp let out a deep, exhausted laugh that came all the way from her stomach. A few seconds passed before she answered.

"No," she finally said. "A baseball."

He glanced at her, down to the mitt in her hand, then back at the hole, and finally pointed at her. Trapp nodded happily. Cleaver mimed a windup and let loose an invisible ball aimed for the same spot.

"Wowie!" he said, falling on his knees. "I can't believe you did that! That's thick lumber—even if it is rotten." He tumbled on his back and kicked his legs into the air, then scrambled to his feet.

"Miss Trapp, I will be honored if you will allow me to attempt to match your feat."

She handed him her ball, and watched him back away

from the barn before winding up again. "I've seen them do this in *Field of Dreams*—have you seen it?" he said, blowing at the ball. Trapp felt she must have been asked this question some twenty-two times by every kid she knew. "Yes, I believe I have," she replied. "And I've also seen *The Music Man*, but that doesn't mean I can sing the songs."

This time, with a real ball, she could see how delicate his arm was. The ball landed far short of the barn. Her heart went out to him.

Cleaver watched the ball roll to a stop, his lips pursed, one eyebrow up. "By the end of the summer."

"What?" Trapp said, coming to stand next to him.

"I said, 'By the end of the summer.' I will try to match your feat by the end of the summer," he said. "Baseball hasn't been—much to the consternation of family, friends, and gym teachers—my game. But I'd like to be better." He turned to her. "You could help me out."

"Sure, if you think I can," she replied.

"Yup," he said. "It's a project. I always have summer projects."

They walked side by side into the barn. Cleaver stopped in delight, staring at the furniture-strewn straw. "All of this is your great-grandpa's furniture?" he asked her. "This is amazing." He walked around the expanse of the barn, running his finger across the tops of chairs, and over the beveled edges of desks. "This is a ladder-back," he said. "And this is a Shaker."

He seemed to know things—like about the hole in the barn wall—and she didn't know how. Cleaver was open

—so animated, and interested. She watched him peer at the spool legs, comparing the fine details, trying to determine what part of a Morris chair had been broken, and what of a Brewster had been reproduced.

She was reminded of her grandpa as she watched Cleaver move from piece to piece. He peered at the carvings on cabinet backs, and the grain of armoires and tabletops, nodding at one piece—"a highboy chest"—shaking his head at another—"a hutch." She marveled again that, as clumsy-looking as Cleaver was, every move was filled with grace—he spun among love seats and whatnot shelves the way a ballerina would twirl among the members of the corps de ballet.

"This Chinese Chippendale looks like a birdcage, really," he said with a chuckle. He was as alert to the intricacies of furniture making and restoration as her grandfather was, only Cleaver's actions betrayed more awe. "This must be the most ancient inglenook I've ever seen," he murmured. Grandpa Hatfield acted a little less deliberate, and always distinctly matter-of-fact. Cleaver mentioned things she'd never heard of, like a "cockfight chair," and a "banjo clock without its bob."

Trapp watched as he ran his hand along the desk where the carving was hidden, and turned her back to him, making her own hands busy with her mitt and ball. Not yet, not yet, she silently wished. It was granted.

"This is just swell," Cleaver said with a deep, satisfied sigh. She turned in time to see him shake his head wonderingly. "We can come again, right?" he asked.

Trapp smiled more broadly than she intended, relieved

that the secret was safe. "Of course," she replied. He beamed. They were silent on the way to the farmhouse. Cleaver kicked at the gravel path, and Trapp didn't feel the need to talk, especially not over the clatter of dish-washing and conversation pouring out the kitchen window as they neared the house.

When the faucet was abruptly turned off, Trapp heard Grandma Eustacia's words clearly: "It's only natural they look like each other. And both so skimpy, too."

Trapp looked at Cleaver. Had he heard, too? *Who* looked alike? Gabby's low answer was indiscernible to her, and Cleaver's face didn't change. Suddenly the screen door swung open and Gabby strode out onto the top step. She looked over her shoulder at Grandma and Grandpa and Don, who all appeared in the doorframe, then faced Trapp and Cleaver, tall and straight. Her eyes were questioning and bright, but her words were casual.

"Ready to go?" she asked Cleaver.

"Yes, if I can come back tomorrow," Cleaver said. "Or if Trapp can come over—do you want to?" he asked her.

"I'll see," Trapp said, curious about the Stuttgards' home. "Is it close enough to ride my bike?"

"I'll drive you and your bike over," Grandpa said. "You wouldn't want to ride both ways, just to see Saratoga here."

"No problem, Mississippi," Cleaver said, smiling at Grandpa. Grandpa winked back. "See you tomorrow, Trapp." He was taking for granted that she would come, and she liked it.

How a country walk down the lane of sugar maples makes everything okay

Trapp looked over Grandpa's shoulder as he painted paste, made from cornstarch, over the backs of old-fashioned greeting cards. His hands were bony and twisted with age. Beneath the whites of his nails—as if it were part of his skin—was a line of what was known as "good farm dirt." His palms were smooth and pink as the cupids' flesh on the valentine cards he was sorting. Carefully printed ink words, written some seventy years earlier, were still clear and crisp.

"You won't be able to read them anymore," Trapp said, touching the fine white hairs barely visible on the backs of Grandpa's hands. "If they're glued down, I mean."

The sides of his nails and cuticles were reddish-brown half-moons, the color of furniture stain he could never entirely wash away, and the middle joints were cracked and dry.

54

He reached up and rubbed his cheek with the back of his gnarled hand. The pads of his fingers were sandpaper-rough and made a scratchy noise against anything he touched. His knuckles bulged and popped beneath his skin, but he showed no signs that it hurt.

"I've read all of them so many times they're committed to memory," Grandpa answered, tapping his eyebrow with one finger. "And I've always wanted to have all my valentines in one big volume." He placed a postcard of a plump Edwardian lady carefully on the page. Using a handkerchief, he rubbed off the paste that oozed out from either side of her when he pressed down.

Trapp still wondered about losing the words. It didn't seem right to cover them up after so many years. Idly she ran her fingers through the stack he was working with, then began to turn them over, reading the words on each.

"Be Mine," she read from one; then picked up another. "Cheri-shable One," it said. "Can't Bee-lieve How Much I Care," said another, sporting a bumblebee. She turned it over. "Love, Gabby."

Trapp sat up straight.

"Grandpa!" she said excitedly. "Is this Gabby Stuttgard?" He looked at it and nodded matter-of-factly. "Yup, she was always a nice girl." He took it from her and painted the back with paste; then pressed it down with determination next to the Edwardian woman.

Staring at him intently, Trapp looked for signs that he was hiding anything about Gabby, about him. But his face was unchanged, although the shock of white hair falling across his forehead shielded his eyes.

55

"Nice girl," he muttered again. Then his eyes lit on another valentine, which he picked up and kissed. "From your grandma. I remember when she gave this to me. She made sure I'd see it by slipping it into a novel I was reading for English—a favorite of mine. I found the card while I was walking home." He read the message on the back, and chuckled as he dabbed paste on the corners. "I might want to look at this one again," he told her. "So I'll just paste it in a *little*."

Trapp was curious to read the card. But she was also busy thinking about his behavior toward the two valentines. "Nice girl" for one, and a kiss and a glow for the other.

But that was how someone *would* act if he was covering up a romance.

Trapp sighed, but not very loud. Grandpa's reaction had seemed genuine. If he had ever liked Gabby, it had been a hundred years ago. But when had the initials been scratched into the desk? And if it wasn't Grandpa that the initials referred to, who was it?

"What was that sigh about?" Grandpa said. "Or did you think these old ears were so useless that I wouldn't hear it?"

"All this old-timey stuff," Trapp said. "You've always lived here. I don't understand why I—why my mom and dad or anyone—should have to move."

"I don't guess I know, Trapp. Don't like it myself." He put his hands on the table, folding one over the other, and craned his neck around to see more of her, closely. "Your daddy says he's got important business to do in the city, and I'm sure he's right. I don't much like treating the land as a commodity, with numbers and charts and such on that Wall Street place—but it appears he does. I guess he'll be taking the high road from here on out. That's all it is, when you really think about it."

"But maybe he would find more business if he stayed where he was," Trapp said.

"Well, maybe that's true. But even an old rooster like me knows that every now and then a man's got to go where the weather vane points." Grandpa's sigh almost matched Trapp's for wistfulness. "When someone makes a decision to move his whole family from one place to another, you've got to figure that he's thought through all his options."

Grandpa closed the album and slowly pushed his chair away from the table. "You have to think about your mother, too, Trapp. They've never had to move anywhere before."

"Neither have *I*," Trapp reminded him again. "I'll have to go to a new school and get stared at and be hated by kids who have grown up together."

"Yes, but your mother is older. She's more set in her ways," Grandpa told her.

"I guess I didn't give it much thought just now," Trapp said.

"Your mother won't have an easy time meeting new friends and neighbors," Grandpa said gently, standing behind her. His voice rang out over her head, and his words seemed to fall on her shoulders like weights. "Your father has a new—well—job, and will know the people he does business with. You children will meet people through school—because, Trapp, no matter what you think, you will make friends, and New York folk, I hear, are no different from any, perhaps even better. It just takes time to find the people you want to know. You have the whole big school to choose from, but remember, you really only want two or three good friends. You can be pretty darn picky."

Trapp tried to shrug his words away. Still he continued.

"Your mother won't find friends at work or school, and she'll have to learn her way around a new city, a larger city," he said. "I don't envy her. In fact, I might even be scared, if it were me."

Trapp squeezed her eyes shut, and tried to picture, just for a minute, her mother in a different grocery store, in a different laundry room other than her own, making a bed in a different house, picking Maggie up outside a different school.

Grandpa was right. But she didn't want to admit it.

Finally she said, "I'm sorry," and felt relieved. "I'm selfish," she added, even though she still wasn't sure she was going to go for the move.

"Never," Grandpa said. "Now I've made you worry about two people instead of just one."

"But I don't feel as bad as I did," Trapp said.

"Well, I guess that's good," Grandpa said. "You want to take a walk on it?"

Her great-grandmother came bustling in. "I think I have to help Grandma with the meal," Trapp said.

"I just made a cheese casserole with the garden vegetables you picked and cleaned for me this morning," Grandma said. "It's in the oven, and you're free for at least half an hour."

"Then let's take a walk—on it," Trapp said. She pushed her hand into her great-grandfather's own. He might be old, but he was smart, and his hand, far from feeble, firmly clasped hers and led her out to the lane.

A dome of leaves overhead shielded them from the hot midday sun. Grandpa's steps on the brown dirt surface were sure, but to Trapp it seemed as if she were hopping and skipping over bumps rather than taking a peaceful country walk.

"These trees are mighty old," Grandpa said. "My grandfather could have planted elms, and then we would have lost them all to that Dutch disease a few years back. But he planted poplars along the fields, and sugar maples here, and so we still have them, and they'll be allowed to grow to a ripe old age."

"Can you get maple syrup from them?" Trapp asked.

"Yes," Grandpa said. "We could, I suppose, if we tried."

"But you never tap them?" Trapp asked. "We learned about it in school."

"I don't think we even considered it," Grandpa answered.

"But you and Grandma are always talking about making use of everything, and of not wasting anything."

"That's true," Grandpa answered. "But we don't have to use up resources just because they're there. Tapping trees would have been extra work all these years, and I was busy with the farm—you remember, I used to raise alfalfa as well as corn, and we were always making runs to the creamery from the cows we kept. And these trees do enough for us—giving us shade, keeping some of the snowdrifts off the road—we don't need more than that."

"I'd like homemade maple syrup," Trapp said, dropping his hand.

"You mean we don't have enough sweets around here for you?" Grandpa asked. "Homemade pies, fudge, divinity, jams?"

"That's not what I mean," Trapp said. "You and Grandma just make everything seem so, well, useful. Syrup sounded useful, too." She kicked at a deep rut, once, then again, and had to run a few paces to catch up to Grandpa.

"Things around here are so old," she said suddenly. "I don't mean you."

Grandpa laughed, deep in his chest, a rumble that meant he was pleased.

"Sure I'm old. So's your grandma. So is this land. So are the stories, and these trees. Even though they're fairly old by tree standards, they shouldn't all be doing so poorly. Don't know why. Something in the air, I suppose." He sat down on a stump, shaded by the maples on either side of him.

Trapp stopped thinking, hearing only the branches wave and hum and whisper overhead.

Her mouth felt dry and dusty. The ancestors' pictures. The faded valentines. The tall trees. Grandpa and Grandma's frailness. "What's old is sad," she finally said. "Because it means it's going to go away."

"What's old is *old*," Grandpa said. "And there is no

way around the fact that some things *do* go away. People, for one. But it isn't sad. You're going away, too. I won't see you very often. And I'll miss you, but I won't be sad."

"I know," she answered. "But I'll still be alive. That's why you won't be sad." She swallowed again. She wanted to cry, but the tears only pressed behind her eyes, making her cheeks and nose ache.

Grandpa took her arms and pulled her into his lap.

That morning, she would have felt too tall for him. Now she let him fold her into his arms, and his words were close to her ear. "When I'm gone," he murmured, "you'll think of me. You'll remember this summer, and all the other times you've been here with me and your grandma. Maybe you'll remember our conversations. Maybe not."

Trapp started sniffling. The tears were moving closer to the surface, and her nose was running.

"Hush, hush," he whispered. "Don't. You'll remember the pies baking, or the smell of corn just off the stalk, or even the scent of rotten wood in the barn. I'll be alive, for you, in those moments. Just as my grandfather is alive for me, every time I walk down this lane of trees."

"Oh, Grandpa," Trapp moaned, curling her arms around his neck. She cried into his soft cotton collar, and into the white hair that waved over his ears. "I don't want to think about it. I don't want you to talk about it," she sobbed.

"We have to, honey, we have to," he told her. "On the farm, you see living and dying all the time. All the time Don't cry."

61

She tried to stay quiet, and hiccuped once. Grandpa's slow, steady breathing was soothing. He felt solid and strong to her. As if he would always be there. Without thinking, she started to wipe her nose dry on his shoulder. Abruptly she stopped.

"That's okay," he said. "I didn't bring a handkerchief —you might as well use my shirt." He patted her back as she slowly eased out of his lap, then helped him to his feet. Grinning, Grandpa rubbed the small of his back and straightened up.

"My lap used to be larger," he said.

"And I used to be smaller," Trapp replied. She held on to his hand tightly.

Limping slightly, he leaned on her shoulder as they walked up the lane. "Seems to me you're just the right height," he said. She nodded and wrapped one arm around his waist.

"Just right," he repeated, and then he said no more, all the way to the farmhouse.

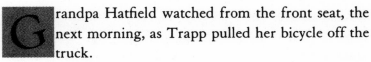

An additional, nearly action-oriented sidetrack concerning throwing up and smelling the flowers

randpa Hatfield watched from the front seat, the next morning, as Trapp pulled her bicycle off the truck.

"Now, don't forget," he told her. "If you're tired from playing around here all day, just phone up and I'll come get you. It's a long bike ride home, and the heat's just billowing off the blacktop."

"Okay," Trapp replied, coming to the truck window. Grandpa kissed the top of her head.

"Well, lookee there, Tucson!" Grandpa said, waving as Trapp turned around. "You don't look half as skinny in long pants."

"Thank you, Mississippi," Cleaver answered. " 'Green's jeans with ease, we aim to please.' Exit—"

"What's that, what's that?" Grandpa declared, without expecting an answer. He rolled his eyes at Trapp. "Call if

63

you need to," he repeated, starting the engine. Then he drove off in a cloud of dust.

"What do you want to see first?" Cleaver asked her, taking her bike and wheeling it toward the Stuttgards' farmhouse with an easy lope. "There's the main house— just like yours—my room, the cellar, the meadow, or the woodshack. Only it's not a woodshack, really."

Trapp, intrigued, said, "What is it if it's not a woodshack?"

"Gabby writes there in the summertime. She's putting together notes from her work."

Trapp shied away and shook her head. "No, I don't need to see that," she replied. "You tell me what's good."

"The meadow," he said quickly. "In the spring it's really something, but even now there are hundreds of different wildflowers blossoming." Despite his long pants, Cleaver was dry and cool-looking as a scarecrow in the heat. Trapp was aware of her own sweaty arms and legs and the perspiration above her lip. For a moment she felt a bit queasy.

She hurried to follow him past the two-story frame house, white, with Chinese-red shutters and window boxes full of pink and red geraniums. It looked cleaner than her grandparents' house, more straight and tidy; the porch, firm and sturdy; and the house was freshly painted.

They began to walk, as she and her grandpa had done the day before. She and Cleaver passed a short tract of woods, alongside yet another expanse of corn. As the clouds hovered above, so did the fields seem to below. You could never get away from them, Rakes would say. Vast lakes of green, huge enough to checker the blue of the sea . . . more corn than there was in China.

No, she couldn't get away from them, and she didn't think she wanted to.

A dark, cool trail within a small, thick forest sent a chill through her. In a twinkle they had stepped out of the shimmering heat of the fields, from a glaring spotlight into a refrigerated glen.

Cleaver sailed effortlessly ahead, the trail rolling along beneath his feet. But Trapp's eyes couldn't adjust to the faint light. She thrashed through the underbrush, unable to see branches until they were thrust right up front. She was lagging farther and farther behind. Then she couldn't see him at all. She brought her arms up in front of her face for protection, and ran, faster and faster, into the crackling, snapping brush. She wanted, she knew it at that moment, to sleep for a very long time. There had been no real signs for it, but nausea suddenly threatened with every step. The food she had eaten for breakfast danced slowly before her eyes against the hazy screen that was all she could see.

Then there was movement ahead, and a figure—it had to be Cleaver. As if in a movie, he appeared and then disappeared from sight, merging into a blurry white arena, a stage with too many lights, just outside the trees.

Trapp couldn't move fast enough. Branches tugged at her hair, but she pushed through the last cluster of trees and stumbled out into the open.

A bright shaft of sunlight made the visions of food dissolve, piercing her sight with an ache that nearly split her head in half. She reached up to hold her head together. Her face was hot, her hands were cold.

Her legs gave out and she was grateful to be sinking to the ground. It was a relief not to be standing, not to be supporting her weight, to feel the grass beneath her knees, and to cough once, and then to throw up the muffins and eggs—"yuck!"—her grandma had insisted she eat that morning.

Again and again she vomited into the green blades so near her eyes that she closed her lids against them.

The sun's direct beam raised goose bumps on her cool, scraped arms. She pulled clean grass toward her and wiped her mouth, belatedly aware that Cleaver was hovering over her.

"Jeez, Trapp," he said. "Jeez. Are you all right?" He sat down next to her, next to—where she'd been sick, and she was embarrassed, and angry.

"Get away from me," she cried. She kept her head forward, refusing to look into his eyes, where she would see his concern—humiliating concern. "Get away," she repeated in a mumble.

"Take it easy," he said, standing up. He seemed to ignore her anger. "Give yourself a minute. Look, I'd bring you water from the stream, but I don't have anything to carry it in. I'll help you to it, and you can wash up."

"I want to go home," she said.

"Nah, you'll be tops in no time," Cleaver told her. "In a bit. Let me help you."

"I said I want to go home," she said, glaring at him. She wiped her sour mouth with the back of her hand.

And for the second time in as many days, she felt tears sting her eyes. Cleaver averted his own gaze. He walked away and sat down in the grass a few steps from her, his back to her.

Her head cleared, and a mild breeze cooled her. It had been so deeply dark it felt she would never come away from it alive. Silly.

"You *are* okay now, aren't you?" Cleaver called over his shoulder. "I'm sorry you were sick, but the heat does that, you know."

"Where did you say the stream was?" Trapp asked, climbing shakily to her feet. Cleaver pointed, but did not stand, did not speak. She only had to walk a few paces before she saw it, a narrow blue rush of water cutting through long green grass.

Leaning down, she splashed her eyes and mouth, and began to feel normal again. The stream water was clear, unsoiled; she could observe the bed, covered with small shiny pebbles, smoothed by the bubbles that passed over them.

Better. She was better. Trapp stood upright again, and swayed weakly as she looked around.

Lying fallow

An exhilarating array of flowers surrounded Trapp on three sides. The only green areas in the entire meadow were beneath her feet, and where Cleaver was sitting.

Squared-off patches of blossoms held wild swirls of purple, yellow, red, and white, dotted with orange, pink, and blue. Some flowers bristled lightly in the wind, others grew still and close to the ground.

Trapp had seen fields of one kind of flower—daisies, or dandelions, or clover—but never so many different flowers in one field, all tidy and starched in uniform patterns.

"What is this place?" she asked, inhaling deeply. She knew, trusted somehow, that Cleaver would ignore the fact that she had said she wanted to go home. She wanted to stay, gazing at the colorful puffs, breathing in the fragrance. Trapp had never known of such a large tract of land going without a cash crop. There was room for a tractor, or plow, but somehow this land was allowed to lie fallow.

"Once this land was bust," Cleveland said. "Nothing survived. As if all the topsoil had blown away." He stood up, and while Trapp watched, he seemed to grow both in height and years before her eyes, as in the slow-motion photography of TV nature programs.

"It looks healthy now," Trapp said. "Why isn't this used for corn?" She felt a little grownup herself.

"Don said he'd have to blaze a trail through the woods, and he never wanted to do that," Cleaver said. "Others told him to get rid of the whole forest, but he wouldn't do that either. And, Trapp, this just looked like a dust bowl—you can't believe how barren it was—not even weeds."

She tried to picture it, to put it in front of her eyes the way she had tried to conjure the ancestors in the barn. "What changed it?"

"*Who* changed it," Cleaver said, correcting her. "It was Gabby."

Trapp smiled. Gabby looked strong, but no elderly woman or man could have tended such a wide-open space. She shook her head, and Cleaver caught her meaning.

"No, really. When their parents died, Don got the farm buildings and the land, and Gabby got the bulk of the money. She was busy at school—in New York. Cornell? Wonder if that's close to where you'll be living?" Trapp shook her head while Cleaver cupped his hands around the stem of a flower and buried his chin in the blossom.

"I guess she always had the money—Don called it living off the interest instead of living off the land—while she finished up, and then some for founding an institute. The Institute for Cross-Fertilization I think Don calls it, or maybe Cross-Pollination." Cleaver paused, thinking.

"When she came back, she sunk a log of money into the planting of this meadow," he continued. "It went for plants and huge crews of people to do soil tests and bring nutrients in, all without large machinery, because there was no road in here. The meadow was full of clover and alfalfa for a couple of seasons, just to give it a leg-up."

All those people, Trapp thought, just to plant flowers. Her great-grandparents always worried about their harvest. Even though they had plenty to pay the crews Rakes brought in, they never knew until the workers showed up if they were going to get the crop in at all. It was so hard for them to manage, at their age, while someone only a few years younger could just breeze in with money, for a field of flowers that was just going to wither and die?

"She replanted wildflowers and brought in some that she said used to be native to the area," he continued. "She likes to say that 'some of the most beautiful flowers grow untended.'"

"But why?" Trapp asked. Cleaver shrugged, but didn't answer.

"Why?" Trapp said again. "Why is this whole field going to waste?"

Cleaver looked at her, startled. "Waste?" he replied. "It never needs to be planted. Well, for a few years it needs a little help—'naturalizing,' Gabby said. After that it will just regenerate itself. Gabby loves this place; she calls it her baby. And you think it's a waste?"

Trapp looked around, silent again in the midst of the striking flowers. Butterflies and birds darted among and over the meadowlands.

But then there were the woods. Her heart had something akin to these woods—something that made her feel too hard, and dim, and sad for her age. As if that rock that had sat in her stomach ever since her mother had told her that they were moving away belonged here, in this meadow just beyond the woods.

It was hard not knowing where home was: where to come to at the end of a day after all was said and done. And seeing people she loved reach the end of the road, and places she loved stand still and not continue along with her into the future.

Trapp felt she'd become too old too soon. The hard place inside had grown, in a very unrocklike manner, ever since she began to realize how old her great-grandparents were, and how many people had lived before them that were now dead, dead and gone, and how they would soon be dead and gone, and how she would someday be dead and gone. All those photos, and the valentines that made her think Grandpa Hatfield had been a boy *yesterday* instead of a million years ago, that was how fast lives passed. He had told her that not everything on a farm had to be useful. But he, and Rakes, and others, mostly were always saying that the land was the only thing that endured, and had to be used well. That corn would be grown made sense to her—it fed people, and animals. But these blossoming, patterned patches, so oddly placed—of what use were they to anyone? It was almost like putting an Easter bonnet on a workhorse, or frosting on whole grain bread. Surely Grandpa didn't mean that it was all right for the sugar maples, or this meadow, to go to waste. People came and went in a wink. The trees and this field had to be the only things that counted, that lasted.

"Things have to mean something," she said to Cleaver, but more to herself. "This is pretty, but it doesn't mean anything. Yes," she said loudly. "This is a waste."

"I don't know why you have to be . . . so difficult and touchy about everything," Cleaver said, backing up and seeming to pirouette. "You're behaving like a grownup and you're only a-a-a kid, like me." His face was hard and set when he turned to her again.

"I suppose your grandpa thinks that unless you can eat it, a crop's no good," he sputtered. "Don's like that, too. He and Gabby have argued over that so much I could spit. But all this"—he waved at the field—"counts, too, and if you can't see that, I'm sorry for you and I'm sorry I brought you here."

Trapp opened her mouth to say that she wasn't finished saying what she had started, what she wanted to say. She had to tell him about moving—about leaving the things she loved—but there was something more, mostly about the words that wouldn't come out. And something about the summer, so full of secrets, and uncertainty, and changes.

Cleveland looked at her. He did resemble one of the

stern, sober faces in the photos in the parlor more than a boy her own age, in whom she had placed so much trust, so soon. His eyes had taken on the murky sepia color of a tintype. The echoes of all she wished to utter rang in her ears. It wasn't that she disliked the countryside. That was the trouble, wasn't it: that she, of all her family, loved home and the farm and didn't want to move. It was this meadow—something about it. Something. Maybe the jagged rock that sat like a glacier in the middle of everything—it didn't seem to belong there, but looked too big to move.

She wanted to yell out what was in her head. At *him*. What was wrong with her? Cleaver was right, she *was* thinking like a grownup; she was intense, "in-tro-spec-tive," just like an adult, making a mountain out of a molehill.

Cool it. Loosen up! Trapp closed her mouth. Perhaps the place was just too unfamiliar—unexpected, like Christmas in July or a baseball diamond in a cornfield.

Cleaver was storming back through the trees. She hurried after him, more afraid of being left behind than of his turning, maybe, and telling her not to follow him.

The gloom in her mind was dispelled by the rays of sun that filtered down through the leaves and dappled the forest floor. Was it brighter because the sun was higher up in the sky? She could see Cleaver clearly ahead of her, could hear him crunching through the undergrowth.

She emerged, only slightly out of breath, next to the cornfield, and lingered there.

She felt wobbly and not eager to face Cleaver again.

When she reached the Stuttgards' yard, he wasn't in sight. Trapp saw Gabby on the porch alone.

"Hi," Gabby said cheerily. She was holding a large crockery bowl against her stomach. She smiled shyly, but then her eyes, behind her glasses, became concerned. "Cleaver looks like a tornado about to touch down, and you're a bit green around the gills. What happened?"

Trapp shook her head. She couldn't tell a stranger what had taken place.

Gabby still stared at her. Even as she walked over to her bike, Trapp knew she wouldn't make the ride all the way to the farm.

Hang it. She was shy around Gabby, not only because she didn't know her, but also because of the initials she had found. Still, she needed the older woman, if only for the smallest of favors.

"I'd like to use your phone, if that's all right?"

"Sure, sure, Eustacia, come on in," Gabby said, holding the screen door open with one hand. As Trapp passed her, she saw that the bowl in Gabby's other arm was empty.

"I was just about to start baking," Gabby said. She'd noticed Trapp's glance. Her leathery skin took on a rosy hue.

"No, that's not true," Gabby admitted. "When Cleaver flew through here shouting something about the meadow, I wanted to look out for you, to see if you had found your way back okay. I just grabbed the bowl, I suppose, to look busy and useful instead of an old woman fretting over either of you. I'm not used to farm props anymore, I guess.

Actually, I was never good with farm props. I sound silly now, don't I?"

Trapp tried to smile. "You don't have to explain," she said. "My great-grandparents get anxious every time I leave their yard—but I'm used to it."

Gabby sighed, and nodded, as she led Trapp to the kitchen telephone. "I guess I don't have any claim on worrying about you," she said. "Not the way they do."

Trapp didn't know what to say. She recalled her grandma's words the day before: "It's only natural they look like each other." None of it made sense to her. Without warning again, the queasiness came back full force.

When Grandpa Hatfield answered the phone at the other end of the line, Trapp only had to say, "Grandpa?" for him to answer that he would be right over.

She hung up, and Gabby felt her head. "You're hot, child, and white. Are you going to be sick?" Trapp shook her head.

"Well, come on into the parlor, and have a lie down. Ralph will be along soon enough." Gabby gave her a gentle push down a dark hallway, musty and vinegary-smelling as was the rest of the house. The fabric of the old sofa felt rough against her legs and arms when she first lay down. But the parlor was quiet and clean. When she rested her cheek against a satin pillow, it made her feel cool all over. Gabby brushed the hair off Trapp's forehead with smooth, dry hands, and stood there for a moment, watching her.

"You probably guessed," Gabby said, searching for words.

"Guessed what?" Trapp hurriedly filled in, nearly sitting up. "I probably guessed what?"

Gabby continued, "Oh, just that Cleveland is a tiny bit sensitive about that meadow of mine."

"That." Trapp sagged into the cushions.

"Yes. And of me," she added.

"He's . . ." Trapp paused. "He's loyal. Very loyal." She finished the sentence, then fell silent.

"Yes," Gabby replied. "I—I like that in a person, and I think you do, too."

Trapp nodded.

"Then you shouldn't be upset with him. Or him with you," Gabby said slowly. "It's really true, life's too short." She turned her back on Trapp and padded away.

Trapp didn't close her eyes. The Stuttgards' parlor, like the Hatfields', was full of old photographs, but they were pinned randomly to a velvet-backed board instead of framed. Trapp faced the board, noticing the faded areas that surrounded new-looking squares of green velvet, marking places that no longer held photographs. Maybe they had been removed, or merely shifted around, in a different grouping.

Some of the photographs were newer, like those of a small, thin, grinning baby—she was sure those were pictures of Cleaver as a little kid. And she recognized the faded color photos of a younger Don, with a woman Trapp didn't know, in a rowboat on a lake. The old portraits appeared to enfold the recent ones, with more stern faces and more farm settings and grain bins. At the bottom, held in place with a safety pin, was a smiling picture of a baby holding a tiny ear of corn. The baby had wide-set eyes and ringlets pulled up in a bow.

Trapp knew it was her Nana Q. There was one just like it in the Hatfields' parlor, alongside the pictures of other, younger children.

Grandpa Hatfield came in just then, just as Trapp was sitting up to take a closer look at the photograph. His breathing was staccato, as if he had rushed to reach her, and he didn't bother saying hello. "How are you feeling?" he asked, sitting down next to her.

"Who is that?" she quickly answered, pointing at the photo. He glanced at it, then back at her. She watched his face, usually hermetically sealed. She'd learned during the weeks before the Move to "read" her parents' faces—sometimes it was all she had to go on.

But Grandpa Hatfield told her the truth. Right away. His face didn't change at all when he said, "You know who that is—it's our Nana Q. Now, how are you doing?"

"But why is her photo here? Why do the Stuttgards have it?" Trapp asked.

"Well, our families have always been close—Nana was always in and out of this house as much as Don's children were in and out of ours. I'm not surprised they have a photograph of her, bless her heart. Let's get you home, youngster."

"Do we have photographs of Don's children?" Trapp asked. "At your house?"

"Probably—sure we do. Somewhere." He shuffled back down the hall toward the kitchen.

They went out the porch door and saw Gabby in the

garden. She waved when she saw them, and called, "Would you like some iced tea in a bit? I'm almost done here."

"That sounds right fittin'," Grandpa Hatfield answered, "but not today, thanks. I want to get this one home before she loses her breakfast."

"I already have," Trapp muttered, climbing into the truck and waiting while Grandpa loaded her bike.

She saw Cleaver leaning out the window of his bedroom on the second floor, watching, without any trace of expression on his face. Then, just as Grandpa backed out of the driveway, Cleaver seemed to surrender to a smile, and waved at her. It was time-lapse photography again— of a storm front; huge clouds rolled away, and the sun seemed to bounce into focus.

Trapp grinned, shaking her head, and waved back.

Their differences were at least partly mended. But the nausea stayed with her as her great-grandfather drove down the road toward home. She went over the past few minutes in her head.

Gabby *had* offered them tea, but that didn't mean she had ever had a crush on Grandpa. Trapp was getting tired of going round and round about those stupid initials.

Trapp wanted to ask Grandpa straight out; but not while he was driving. For one thing, he tended to swerve in whatever direction he looked in. If he turned to her during conversation, it was likely that the truck would go off the road.

She would wait. And she would try to figure out a way to ask. But when she imagined asking the question—just straight out phrasing a question and watching Grandpa's face as she asked it, her stomach lurched, and she knew she would stay silent.

Whatever the truth was, she wasn't ready to hear it. Yet.

Scarecrows peppered the fields; so did the crows

Insects buzzed in the nearby fields. The wind poured over and rustled sturdy trees. And the kitchen screen door occasionally slammed as Grandma Hatfield snipped and gathered herbs from her garden and carried them inside. These were the only noises Trapp heard.

The distant hum of the highboy drifted her way periodically as Rakes gave the fields an end-of-July spray, before rootworms matured into beetles, and succeeding the first round of insecticides that had been applied in May.

It had been days since Trapp had been at the Stuttgards', and for that time the plaguing stomachache had lingered. It was too warm to nap in her bedroom, but at least she had made it through her chores.

Trapp and her great-grandfather sat under the oak in

the early afternoon, the stillest part of the day. A ladybug crawled up Grandpa's chest as he nodded off in the chair. Its progress was precarious. Gossamer wings burst out from beneath the bright orange protective shields to help it balance in the breeze.

Trapp felt vaguely criminal for allowing an insect— even one as amiable as a ladybug—to insinuate itself on someone who was sleeping, defenseless. Her eyes made the journey between the ladybug's path and Grandpa's face. She noticed that he hadn't shaved for at least two days. Bright-white shoots of stubble marched over the lower half of his face, normally smooth and pink and clean. If only she could take a photograph of him just now, and carry it with her everywhere she went; or better yet, if only she could draw.

Hardly breathing, she lifted her hand and ran the back of it along his unshaved cheek. She heard only a rasping sigh.

Grandpa slowly opened and closed one eye and, with the barest upturn of one side of his mouth, sank back into his doze.

With Grandpa's every breath, Trapp saw gray hairs quiver slightly under his nostrils, and, even in the shady light, the tiny red veins that mottled his cheeks and forehead. His skin looked healthy and glowing—very unlike old photographs. Up close, he had overgrown eyebrows and odd lines and furrows and freckles that were magnified to her lingering zoom.

A mayfly—something that looked like a mayfly but

wasn't—hovered around his head, then quickly moved on. Trapp sat up, and looked Grandpa over. He was breathing steadily.

He seemed so far away. Like a prayer, she tried to conjure up well-known, well-loved signs of him: his dark eyelashes, glossy and gleaming even in the oldest, most faded photos she had held; the soft lips that had whispered, before she had learned to read and ever since, the words of the newspapers and valentines and weather reports, or stuff that seemed out of *The Old Farmer's Almanac*; the white wings of hair, arching across his ears.

Her great-grandfather grunted once and opened both eyes wide. His head rolled toward her on his neck, loose and limber and not ancient at all, and he gave her a real smile, so full of recognition that she believed for a moment that she had found that distant place he was in, and had led him home by the hand, from a light nap or from some much greater patch of land.

"I'm supposed to keep you company while you rest," Grandpa said, right off. "But it looks like you're playing some sort of scarecrow angel instead. Or maybe the corn fairies got me."

Trapp ducked her head, blushing. She felt foolish, like a balloon slowly deflating. He clicked his teeth a couple of times, setting them straight as he worked his jaw around. He brought his hand up to shade his eyes as he looked off in the distance.

"What's the date?" he said.

Trapp told him.

"Yup! Right on schedooly-o," Grandpa Hatfield said. Trapp followed his gaze and saw a large green van coming their way. She had dreamed about such a van—a real dream, a large moving truck coming in to take her possessions away and sailing through a fast lane to the new place. It had big purple letters, PYLGRIMM & CO., blasted on its side. Her heart speeded up.

She watched the truck's progress down the lane of sugar maples. At home, where the street passed by the front of the house, she would have ignored such traffic. But here there was only one route to the farm, and no other place for the truck to go than to their front door.

Grandpa Hatfield glanced down at Trapp. "Never fails to surprise me how another year goes round," he told her. "That truck—seems like it poked on over here yesterday morning. And now here it is again."

The truck was close enough for Trapp to read the lettering. The red-and-white sign on its side said SALVATION ARMY in tall letters. It rolled over the grass of Grandpa's front yard, then stopped, and with the skill of a driver far more accustomed to dirt roads than superhighways, headed rapidly backwards in the direction of the Hatfield barn.

Grandpa shuffled away from the oak and looked back at Trapp. "Think if I move slow enough, those two sprouts in the front seat won't make me work?" he asked her. She nodded, but couldn't grin, then settled in to watch.

With a theatrical flair that Trapp associated more with

Cleaver than an elderly man, Grandpa put one hand on his hip, bent over slightly, and hobbled off toward the barn.

She gasped.

"What's wrong, honey?" asked Grandma, catching the sorrowful look on Trapp's face. She had crossed the yard so quietly that Trapp hadn't even noticed her coming, and handed over a small blue bowl of blackberries.

"He looks too real," Trapp whispered, taking the bowl. "Too frail."

Grandma just smiled fondly at her husband's retreating form. "No need to go all long in the face," she said. "And since when did you start seeing life from a fishpond full of dead guppies, Eustacia?" She patted Trapp's knee and left her alone under the tree.

As if to confirm Grandma's chiding, Grandpa turned and winked straight at Trapp. The joke of his posture sank in, and Trapp lowered her head to laugh, afraid the truckers would think she was making fun of them. She took a berry and bit into it. "Thanks, Grandma," she called.

The barn would soon be empty, she knew. Of course, it had been empty for years, but for the jars and the furniture and the various trinkets—but now Grandpa would piece by piece put new dressers, desks, chairs into the dusty straw to replace those that the men were taking away. She didn't want to watch, to see the desk with the hidden initials in among the other objects, didn't want to think of the secret—whatever it was—being whisked, after all these years, from one small place into a much larger one.

She moved from the tree to the porch until she heard the truck start up.

Soon Grandpa was striding back, walking like his old self as the van moved off down the lane.

"That was a big job," Grandpa said. "Is it possible I'm spending more time on the silly woodwork than I am on this farm?"

"Maybe from year to year you forget how much work you've done," Trapp suggested.

"Oh, I know that's true, Trapp," Grandpa said, sitting next to her with a *harrumph*. "Planting and harvesting. Planting and harvesting. If I remembered all the jobs I'd done—all the tasks I've just repeated over and over—I might come up feeling pretty useless."

"No," Trapp said, her voice steady.

"Yes," Grandpa said. "Yes." He was silent for a while. "But that's just a piece of it. Those runaway tables and chairs may do good. The rows I've hoed, the mounds I've planted—they gave me a family, and my family has *its* family, and we've always had more than plenty, and some in the bank. That's not nothing."

"Right," Trapp said. "So don't use words like 'useless' anymore." She couldn't meet his stare.

"Well, what has you all upside down with the willies?" he asked. Trapp didn't answer. "Trapp? You afraid I'm going to be mad about that bite you took out of my barn wall? I'm as giddy about a good pitch as the next fella."

"Oh, be quiet, Ralph," Grandma said, stepping out to the porch. "I know why Eustacia's bothered. I always feel sad when that furniture rumbles off each year. You don't know where it's going to end up. And it sort of marks the season's passing—winter is almost here."

"Winter!" Grandpa said. "By golly, you both are pushing us into a blizzard when we haven't even got to harvest yet." He stood up, hitched his pants, and stuck his hands in his pockets. "What's wrong with today, I'd like to know? And that furniture—well, I think of a family gathering around a solid oak table instead of that formal-gee-hidie plastic stuff, and I feel pretty darn pleased. Pretty darn pleased, yessir."

"This is a very respectable meal," Rakes said solemnly to Trapp, poking his fork through a thick slice of roasted meat.

The summer rain that had pelted the crops all day long had subsided to fitful drips outside the steamed-up windows.

"Grandma fixed the roast," Trapp willingly offered. "She pounded three kinds of meat till they were flat out, then wrapped all of them up like a jelly roll around the parsley."

"Oh, but you did tend it all day long and add the vegetables at the right moments," Grandma told her, standing up. "That's how I learned to make a three-way roast when I was newly wed, hardly much older than you are now." With thumb and forefinger she whisted a sputtering candle on the windowsill.

"That's the truth of it," Rakes said, nodding over his plate. "That's how she learned."

"How would *you* know?" Trapp asked.

"I would know," Rakes replied. "I remember about that. And about the husking bees she used to host, and . . . lots of things." He turned his face toward the window, listening. A fluttering noise of stirred-up gravel could faintly be heard.

Grandpa was chewing silently.

"You aren't old enough," she persisted.

"Well, then just say that I remember my father—or maybe it was my grandfather; sitting here as I am now, it makes no difference—telling me about a lady coming to the farm as a bride," he said. "Time flies faster than it takes to cook a meal."

Grandpa was looking out the window, still chewing.

Grandma gave Trapp a head-on smile. With her apron, she rubbed away a patch of steam on the glass. "Someone's at the door." Grandma's words were followed by the brisk scratching of boots on the welcome mat, and a knock at the screen door.

Trapp turned around to see Cleaver stomping into the kitchen. He carefully shed his damp raincoat and made a few swipes at his wet hair, trying to put it back in place.

Other than that last formal motion, he seemed as at home in the Hatfield house as Trapp was. She was surprised to see him—they hadn't spoken to each other since the day in the meadow. Trapp wondered if she needed to apologize, if only to say that she didn't know why she had acted so badly.

88

"Good to see that old Santa Fe here still knows how to drop in on people properly," Grandpa said.

"We finished up supper an hour ago and I biked over —um, I thought I would—er, yes, drop in," he told them. He motioned toward Trapp awkwardly. "The rain's let up and the sky's lighter; there's still plenty of daylight if you can—maybe practice some ball or—"

She shook her head, but didn't want to send the wrong message. "I promised to help set up the quilt frame after we ate."

Cleaver put down his mitt next to the mat. "I'll help or whatever," he said. "If you're finished eating, that is."

"I'm finished," Trapp said. "Cleaver and I will do the quilt frame."

Grandpa wiped his mouth with a napkin. "Oh, you can go on," he said. "We won't need that for a bit." Grandma waved them away.

"I'll drive you home later," Rakes said to Cleaver.

"Thanks," Cleaver said. He and Trapp were out of the house in two beats.

"About the other day—" Cleaver said, as soon as they were out of the adults' hearing.

"Don't," Trapp said. "It's my fault, and I'm sorry."

The path to the barn was slippery with mud, bordered by damped-down grass. Cleaver plowed right through every puddle that dotted it.

"Gabby said you were ill, and that it was my fault for not taking better care of you," he replied.

"No," she said. "It's no excuse. I'm sorry."

"I'm sorry, too," he said.

"Okay," Trapp said, "I accept your apology if you accept mine."

"Done," Cleaver said, holding out his mitt.

"Done," she replied. "If only we can get to play some ball."

"We'd better get right to it," Cleaver said. He wiped a raindrop from his cheek. "It's getting ready to come down on us."

The game of catch was hampered by a real downpour and the onset of darkness. They were both drenched and breathless from the chase back to the farmhouse.

"Summer is passing so quickly that I don't have much time to get my practice in," Cleaver said between huffs. "The days are already short."

At the door, Grandma handed each of them a towel. The smell of fresh buttered popcorn filled the kitchen. "I won't have any chilblain cases on my hands," she said.

She and Grandpa had settled into the parlor for the evening. Rakes was nowhere to be seen.

Cleaver sat on the floor, his back to a high Victorian couch. Grandma dismissed his offers to help with the frame, and put a bowl of popcorn in his lap. Trapp helped Grandpa get the wooden form set up before taking her place on the couch.

"Gabby's had an offer on her house," Cleaver told them.

Grandpa and Grandma sat over the quilt and put the first stitches into an expanse of nine-square patches. An overhead light blazed down on their work, wrapping them in brightness. The rest of the parlor was dim, perked up only by occasional lamps.

"Her house, honey?" Grandma asked. "Surely you don't mean her New York place?"

"That's the one," Cleaver replied. "She says her lawyers have written her about a good deal."

She tried to look into Grandpa's face at this news, but he never looked up from his needlework. The rain continued a steady beat on the windowpanes. Trapp was content to swing her legs, letting the others talk.

"You suppose that means she's moving back here for good?" Grandpa asked, to no specific person. Thunder rumbled, low and far off.

"Maybe for summers. I don't think so," Cleaver replied. "A family's moving in, but she'll still have a garden apartment. All the stairs in the rest of the place were wearing her out, I guess. Especially the ones up to her research room."

"Winding down, it appears," Grandma Hatfield said. "We've all faced it at some time."

"Ho! I'd like to see you wind down!" Grandpa answered. He snipped at the thread he had just knotted and met Grandma's eyes. She blushed, but her needle's plunk, as she pushed it through the layers of batting and cloth, was her only answer.

Cleaver turned to Trapp, disappointment on his face. "You should have moved to New York years ago, when Gabby was there all the time for me to visit."

"Thanks a lot," Trapp told him. "I'm sorry it wasn't more conveniently planned." She sounded more serious than she had intended. She was so accustomed to the idea of not moving away that she had forgotten no one else knew of her plan. But Cleaver, accustomed by now to her gruffness, didn't even flinch.

"That's not the right answer," he said. "What you're supposed to say is 'Then you'll just have to come visit *me*, instead.' "

"Then you'll just have to come visit me, instead," Trapp dutifully responded.

"Nope," he said, standing up and moving toward the hallway. "It will have to be sincere when you say it. You know, a little more from the old beateroo." He knocked on his chest before he and the Hatfields exchanged good nights.

"Rakes will take you," Grandma reminded him.

"Nah, don't bother him," Cleaver said. "He who travels fastest rides by night—even on a wet night." He bowed as Trapp added her own soft "Goodbye" to the chorus.

"Ralph," Grandma said suddenly and irrelevantly, without lifting her head from her work. "Ralph, the downstairs tub is acting all plugged up again. Meant to tell Rakes earlier, but I just didn't get around to it."

"I'll get the Red Devil lye out in the morning," Grandpa murmured over his work, "and put that tub in its place."

Through the window behind the couch, Cleaver appeared on his bike. Lightning broke up the sky, and he was a lone rider, bent over his handlebars. His raincoat flapped around his legs as he pedaled down the lane of maples, and then, in a last flash, out of sight.

Trapp continued to look out the window, long after Cleaver had disappeared. The room had subsided into silence. Trapp curled into the corner of the couch, gratified again for the peace that Grandma and Grandpa deemed a desired part of their evenings. No chatter, no questions, just the sound of their fingers, the bite of the needles, and an occasional squeak of thread against cloth. So much time to think. She couldn't knock out of herself the feeling that whatever lay beyond the fields of corn was too big for her. Or that she was too small still.

Birds made their twilight sounds

From her bedroom window, Trapp saw Grandpa fill up a bucket of water from the garden faucet and dump it over his head. Once again, she had been trying to sleep off her queasiness.

Grandpa shook himself, tooth to tailbone, like an old hound, flinging water everywhere.

Trapp went downstairs, found some ice and a glass, and fixed up some gingerade before heading him off at the back door. He was grinning mischievously.

"In my early years," he said as soon as he saw her, "this would be a day for high-straddling ourselves out over the creek on an old piece of rope. It's just too hot for the fields. Don't know how Rakes stands it." He took the gingerade from her, pulling the liquid down his throat in one swallow.

"Can I help?" Trapp said, taking the empty glass from him.

He shook his head. "I'm almost done for the day—Rakes let me off the hook. You better?"

"Almost," she said. "But I want to do something."

"You promise me you'll stop if you get too hot?" Grandpa asked. "All right, then, you take a pitchfork to that heap of compost—it hasn't had visitors for a while, and it's probably feeling lonely."

"Sure," she said. He had given her an easy job. "Sit by me in the shade, just till some of this heat backs off."

"Maybe I will," he said, walking with her to the rear of the garden. "Maybe I will. Where's that boy today?"

"Cleaver? He and Don went to the co-op in the next town," she told him. "Cleaver has convinced Don that it's time to investigate organic fertilizer. It's better for the soil." She planted her foot on the pitchfork and leaned into it, loosening and lifting up the compost with a shake and then turning it over into the next bin.

"Smelling horse manure," Grandpa said, watching her. "That's the closest I ever come to investigating organic fertilizer. Funny how old ideas come round again."

Trapp gave a short barklike laugh, and pushed the pitchfork back into the compost.

"I like the old ways," she said with a grunt. "But I think it's good Cleaver's trying new things."

"Yes, you do like the old ways, and so does that boy, I bet," Grandpa Hatfield said. "But you got too many whys inside you to apply 'em to farm work. Both of you have curious minds. But his is all locked into the soil, and yours is like a shooting star—got to get beyond the horizon, see what's what. Neither way is better or worse than the other—it takes all kinds.

"Time to face up to composts, horse manure, and a bit of the truth," he added.

"No," Trapp replied, digging deep into the pile and letting loose the warm, earthy scent from beneath the layers. "I don't want to be curious about anywhere else. I just like it here."

"What you want to be and what you are sometimes don't turn out to be the same row to hoe," Grandpa Hatfield told her. "Your grandma and I have talked many times about you, Trapp. You love this place, you'll take it with you, but you'd never stay here, let it hold you back. It's just not the way you work."

"It could be," Trapp insisted. "You don't know that."

"Oh, no, I don't really know," Grandpa said. "It's just the opinion of a tired old soul. But I've seen who can stay around here. Some belong here and nowhere else—even if they don't know it. And I've seen the ones who have to go away—even though they may not know they want to. Good folk, either way. But people usually end up doing what they've got to do, or being what they've got to be. No use going against nature. You about done there?"

Trapp nodded, and Grandpa waited while she pulled the pitchfork out of the last piece of turned-over compost. It was fluffy and aromatic, ready all over again for Grandma's kitchen scraps and garden cuttings.

Sweat was stinging her eyes, and Trapp wiped at them

fiercely. Grandpa didn't know everything, she was certain. But she was having trouble recalling a time when he'd been wrong.

"Looks like it's my turn to go fix you a gingerade," Grandpa Hatfield said, standing up. "In the meantime, why don't you dump a bucket of water on your head? Guaranteed refreshment," he added, and walked on stiff legs toward the kitchen.

"Grandma," Trapp said the next day, picking up a dish and wiping it dry, "did we get mail?" She had slept through one whole night, but the stomachache had been with her all day, and even doing the supper dishes didn't feel entirely normal.

"Yes, honey, but there wasn't anything from your folks." Grandma poked at a cake pan with a wooden spoon, sinking it in the sudsy water. "I'm sure they'll write soon." Trapp knew that it was true—her mother always wrote eventually. Their weekly phone calls were nice, but she preferred a letter—something she could carry around.

"When do you think they'll come here?" Trapp asked. Somehow that question was easier to ask than almost anything else she could think of.

"Just as soon as they can," Grandma answered airily. "You know that, Eustacia. I hope you know that."

"I think they're used to not having me around," Trapp grumbled. Even though she still had no intention of joining them in New York, it was peculiar how much she minded that they didn't seem to miss her. And she wanted to see them. "I think they're waiting until the last minute."

"If they were doing that," Grandma answered, "they would have a good reason for it, and just because you don't know the reason doesn't mean it's not there." She turned off the gas under an old gray kettle and, wrapping a towel around its handle, poured the water over a pile of clean pans.

"Is that to sterilize them?" Trapp asked, glad to change the subject.

"Nope—hot water dries faster than cold," Grandma replied. "So sometimes I give these big pots a last hot rinse, and we'll be able to put them away lickety-split—without wearing out our old arms drying them."

Trapp held out her arm, along the length of the older woman's. Grandma's was sinewy, not really flabby, and her hands were firm and smooth and ready to plunge into bread dough for kneading. Abruptly Trapp put her nose to Grandma's forearm, breathing in the scent of her skin —part scented hand lotion, part soap, part sunshine. Then she raised her eyes, startled.

"You smell like a baby!" she said.

"Sure, sure," Grandma told her. "Grandmas and babies all smell alike." She picked up the pan of leftover peach crisp and put tinfoil across the top. Trapp admired the look and taste of the crisp, not only because of its tart flavors, but because all the ingredients were right there, in the open, almost instantly identifiable. She could see the cinnamon and nutmeg, right there, barely freckles on the peaches' pinky-orange flesh; some of the flour was still white, and powdery; the brown sugar never entirely dissolved.

Trapp loved it the way she loved Grandma's chubby face—nothing was hidden away beneath the surface, or stirred up beyond recognition like a three-day-old hash of beef stew. When Grandma talked to her, Trapp didn't deliberate whether or not she was hearing the truth. Grandma's eyes, of sharp-shooter blue, peered right at her, watched the work she was doing, or scanned in the distance for signs about the weather, but never veered, or shifted, or shied away. Trapp could trust her the way she trusted a peach crisp—the same every time.

Grandma wiped her hands on a dishcloth and plucked a bottle of cornhusker's lotion from the back of the sink. She applied a dab, then offered Trapp a squirt. Silently they worked the clear oil into their hands.

Grandma pulled Trapp closer to her by the pigtail, and held her around the shoulders as they went out to the porch. Trapp saw, not for the first time, how the screens that enclosed it for so many years had turned slightly orange with rust.

Grandpa rocked in the chair he always claimed was older'n *he* was. He had lined up some oil lamps on one ledge, which he usually lit after sundown.

Trapp liked the porch best during rainstorms, when the lamps glowed through a mist-filled air—the screens kept out bugs, and raindrops, but not the moisture.

"What's that you're looking at?" Grandma said to him, pushing her own chair next to his. He was bent over a photograph, the twin of the one Trapp had seen at the Stuttgards'. Her Nana Q.

"She was a cute child," Grandpa said. "We were so

lucky to get her." His voice rippled over the words, as if they held unleashed tears.

"That we were," Grandma replied, rocking quietly next to him. "That we were." Their voices were soft, mute, like lamplight in the mist, and as their murmurs flowed over her, Trapp didn't want to add her words to theirs. She stood by the sill and stared out at the fields, just beyond the outbuildings and the corncribs. Birds made their twilight sounds.

She missed her parents, and Maggie, and Sam. For a long time she had been missing Nana Q. But mostly—oh, and it came over her like a shudder from a chilling wind—all the missing to come.

All the missing to come.

Her Grandpa and Grandma Hatfield—she knew what missing them was going to be like when they were no longer around, not here, not anywhere. It was brief this time. It left her breathless. But the pain was real enough. How would she ever face it? How did grownups ever face it? Leaving loved ones behind. Not seeing them again— ever again. And it was cruel, too, that she could almost mourn them while they were still here, still next to her. She knew how faces could be empty, eyes staring at nothing—helpless.

"Eustacia, honey, what's wrong?" her grandma asked. As Trapp turned at the sound of her voice, she saw that the old woman was struggling out of her chair. "Child! Are you cold?"

"No, I'm fine, Grandma," Trapp said. "Don't get up."

She patted Grandma back into her chair, and leaned over to give her a hug.

She sat down on the floor between their chairs and drew her knees close to her chest as her grandpa lifted the glass on each oil lamp and lighted the wick. The outside farm faded from view as the closed-in porch began to glow. The crickets could still be heard, and farther away, by a drinking pond for animals, the frogs.

Night was on the other side of the screens, warded off by lamps and the sound of her great-grandparents' voices, tallying the day's activities. Trapp could imagine the beavers working to dam a small stream, from whatever stalks they'd stolen, despite Rakes's careful watch.

Something prodded her, something small, and the murmuring made her brave, and thinking about a time when Grandpa and Grandma wouldn't be around gave her even more courage, and there were too many half-answered questions and half-stated ideas and she was tired of feeling sick and of being scared of hearing answers and she blurted out the one thought that had never been far from her mind, that she hadn't known till now how to ask.

"Grandpa, did Gabby love you?"

If she had been hoping that Grandpa would look surprised or startled or somehow taken aback, and if she had hoped to glean some truth from his reaction, those hopes vanished.

He nodded. And stopped. And slowly nodded again.

"Yes, she liked me, I guess, but I was a good ten years older, and married to your grandmother," he said. "I guess

Gabby always looked up to us because we were in the habit of doing her favors—she'd get into scrapes, and we were just enough older to bail her out, but not as old as her parents—not enough to fuss over her or punish her."

"What kind of favors?" Trapp persisted.

"Oh, lots of little things," Grandpa said. "If she needed a few dollars, she would come to us before she'd go to her own parents, and if she needed someone to cry on, why, your Grandma Hatfield had the best shoulder in the county."

"So you always did—you did neighborly things for her," Trapp added.

"Sure, that's what it's like out here," Grandpa said. "People can't run off and pay someone to listen to their troubles the way they do in the big cities. You have to look to your neighbors, in good times and bad."

"What kind of bad times did Gabby have—I mean, really bad?" Trapp asked.

"Why do you ask, Eustacia?" Grandma said, placing one hand on Trapp's thin shoulder. "What is it?"

Then she remembered—they had said "get" about their daughter—that they had been lucky to "get" her.

People didn't talk about babies like that.

People said "have babies." Not "get babies."

Trapp felt the words rising in her, and knew they were about to gush out of her mouth, about the initials, and about "them" looking alike, and about Gabby saying she had no claim on Trapp, and about the baby photo of Nana Q in the Stuttgards' house, and about Grandpa and Grandma saying that they were lucky to "get" the baby, and all of a sudden, all her queasiness vanished and she knew the answer—and it was such a big answer that she knew it was going to change her life, but she had to ask to see if she had it right. And it had nothing to do with Gabby loving Grandpa, and everything to do with her very own family, with the lives of her mother and her grandmother and her great-grandfather braided together by—God knew what—and what she was left with, all she had to offer, was not a torrent of words. It was one last question.

"Was Nana Q adopted?"

And now. Now she had the reaction she had hoped for from them—a stunned silence, Grandpa clearing his throat, Grandma's eyes suddenly shiny.

"Well—" Grandpa started to say.

"Ralph, let *me*," Grandma said. "Yes she was, Trapp. How did you know?"

"Doesn't matter how she knew," Grandpa interrupted. "I bet all the signs are there—our first visitor to stay over such a long time."

"How did you know, honey?" Grandma repeated.

"Lots of things," Trapp whispered. "I just—just put them in one place, I guess."

"We're almost outta here," Grandpa admitted, "for good." Grandma took out a handkerchief and wiped at her nose, dabbed one cheek, didn't talk.

Grandpa did. "Maybe we get looser with secrets when we get older—things just sort of seep out. An old husker like me can't keep 'em bottled up, and if it leaks, well, there's no secret that seems very big when you don't have much time left. Maybe your grandma and I haven't been as careful as we once would have been, and maybe it just doesn't matter anymore."

Trapp was hardly listening to him. Only when the question was out of her mouth did she realize what the answer might mean to her. If Nana Q was adopted, that meant that Trapp's mother and her children were also adopted. It meant, Trapp saw suddenly, that she wasn't really a great-grandaughter to the Hatfields at all. She didn't belong at the farm, not with them, not anywhere.

The lamplight faded and Grandpa's voice became low, as if the sound had been turned down, and the floor of the porch beneath her, first cool and flat and solid, gave way to a velvety blackness of no-more-questions, blank and comforting and silent.

Kisses covered Trapp's forehead, her cheeks, her chin, and her hands, both her hands. But the world was slow to come back into view. It was reduced to those kisses, hisses, and warmth within a cloudy, frosted window through which nothing was clear. Her vision was unfocused. Whispers. And rocking.

For one long moment Trapp couldn't see, and then in the next, she could—first Grandma's face appeared, and then Grandpa's. She heard his voice first.

"Is she okay, is she better? Does she have a bump?"

"Hush, Ralph, she's fine. A shock, that's all—I forgot how hard a child takes things." Trapp's body felt twisted; then she realized that she was gathered into Grandma's lap.

"How did you pick me up?" she asked, almost hoarse from the pain choking her throat. "I'm too big for you."

She slowly rewound her memory, back to what they had been talking about before the silence, before everything left her.

"Sh, sh, sh, you're a flimsy thing," Grandma said, "and I'm pretty strong for my age—especially when I see a little girl of mine in trouble."

"Am I? Am I a little girl of yours?" Trapp asked, tears falling out of her eyes and back into her hair. "I mean, if Nana Q was adopted, then I guess I don't really belong . . ." She couldn't talk. Her mouth could not form the words. She closed her eyes again.

"Not belong! To us?" Grandpa said, his voice stern. "You're as much a part of us as your Nana Q was, and she was our daughter—couldn't have been more so, may she rest safely. Now, why don't we all talk about this in the morning, when our minds are fresh?"

"Ralph Hatfield! This girl needs some good answers more than she needs sleep," Grandma said. "Can you walk?" she asked Trapp, who had opened her eyes. Trapp nodded. "Then let's go into the kitchen for something hot—yes, something *hot*, Ralph, to soothe her tummy—to drink, and we'll talk there."

The bright overhead light in the big farm kitchen was warm, real, and comforting after the flickering light of the porch. Trapp sank down into the slatted wood chair while Grandma bustled around the stove and poured milk into a pan to warm.

Grandpa pulled out mugs from the cupboard and pushed a plate of cupcakes across the table toward Trapp.

Soon a steaming mug of hot milk was in front of her, sweetened with store-bought maple syrup. She sipped it and watched Grandma make steady, familiar motions: filling the used pan with cold water, giving the sink a quick wipe with a rag, drying her hands on the towel hooked over the refrigerator handle, and then rubbing her hands together. Grandma's hovering was as reassuring as the drink. Trapp settled into the chair and relaxed while she waited for them to start talking.

Grandpa took *his* time to pop some corn, as he'd done a thousand other times. He sat next to her, examining each piece, turned inside out, as if looking for its cause of expansion. "Popcorn always shows you what it's made of," he muttered. "Did I ever tell you the story of the corn seed that popped all the way to New York?" Grandpa jested. Then he withdrew the question. Trapp was glad he didn't make any more jokes.

Grandma finally sat down, and they were all silent. Then she drew a deep breath, and began to talk, rapidly at first but then more slowly, as she wound down a path of memories.

"Gabby Stuttgard was a scrappy young woman," Grandma said. "She should have been sent off to college when she finished high school—she was smart and quick, and life around here was too slow. Oh," she said, staring at Trapp, "we love the farm, and we love our little town, but it wasn't right for Gabby, and"—she looked back at Grandpa—"it wasn't for others. But I'll tell you about that in a minute.

"Lots of the boys around here were sent to agricultural schools, but not the girls. So someone like Gabby—who had read every other book in the school library by the time she was eighteen—didn't have much to look forward to. And she sometimes got into trouble. Plenty of it."

"Like what?" Trapp said, sitting forward in her chair.

"I wouldn't call falling in love—as you'd call it—'trouble,'" Grandpa interrupted.

"No, no, that was the best thing that happened to Gabby," Grandma said. "And to us. She'd been a girl who had never listened to anyone, let alone her parents. But when she fell—that is, when she pledged her heart to a young man, a person she had grown up with, she straightened right out."

Trapp involuntarily glanced at Grandpa. He seemed calm. Then Grandma knew Gabby had been in love with him? Maybe it was similar to what he had said about secrets . . . he was so old that nothing seemed important anymore. Not even an old love.

"You should have seen her in those days," Grandma said to Trapp. "She was pretty, and strong, and in love— why, there were probably a lot of men around here who wondered why they had never noticed her before. But she only went for the one man, and she never looked anywhere else."

Grandpa blew his nose suddenly, and Trapp saw he was weeping almost soundlessly. She felt stuck to her chair, afraid to make him cry harder, afraid to stay where she was.

Grandma reached over to pat him on the shoulder, and wiped away a tear herself. She nodded fast, and hard, as if trying to shake away the next few words.

"Yes, yes, she loved him. And they had plans to go away to school together—he was going to help her in her studies." Trapp was shocked and still—Grandpa had been married, but he was going to leave Grandma for Gabby?

"This young man, his heart had never been in farming. He was like Gabby: the country wasn't big enough for him, wanting something more than the land, and the plowing, and the harvest, and the prairies. He'd been reading about things like Lewis and Clark's ventures beyond Iowa, and such stuff."

Trapp pushed away her now-cold milk. Her stomach churned, thinking of how unhappy Gabby and Grandpa had probably made everyone around them, and thinking of Grandpa as someone who hated the farm.

"Your Grandpa and I have never discussed this, but maybe the accident came out of that discontent about the farm."

Grandpa nodded, and blew his nose again. "I'm sure you're right. No one who loved the farm, who knew what it all meant, would have been that careless."

Grandma continued. "I knew that Gabby was going to have a baby, but I don't think anyone else did. I saw the signs, but kept my mouth shut. So you have to figure that their plans to go away had something to do with that. And that school, if they thought they were going, was probably out of the question. What they needed to do was to get married. Fast."

"But you said there was an accident," Trapp said hurriedly. "What happened—when?"

"He was such a daydreamer, never could keep his mind set on a task," Grandma said. Her voice got low. "A horse spooked and pulled a plow over him. If he'd been paying attention, maybe he could have brought the animal under control. As it was, well, the horse stayed clear of him, but he was—oh, what's that darn word—he was brained by the heavy metal of the plow. And it killed him."

"He?" Trapp said. "Who's *he*?" Lost. She was lost. She didn't understand.

Grandpa reached into his back pocket and pulled out a leather wallet of photographs. Trapp had never seen it before.

He pushed a picture across the table at her, worn and frayed around the edges, but with the two boys in it still visible. She had never seen it before, but she recognized the taller boy from other photos: Grandpa Hatfield as a young man, wearing an oversized hand-knit sweater and a cap pulled down over one eye.

"Who is the boy?" she asked, eyeing the younger person who stood with Grandpa Hatfield's arm around him. He was laughing into the camera, his mouth open, almost as if he were about to take a bite of it, one eyebrow higher than the other.

"Someone you've never seen before?" Grandpa asked.

"Never," she said. "Not in all the photographs in the parlor, not anywhere."

"He's my younger brother," Grandpa said. "Rennie." He smiled and shook his head. "Aw, Rennie. A good brother."

Trapp was beginning to see, but Grandma kept talking, filling in the details.

"Gabby was near dead herself from the grief, and of course, there was the baby. Her parents—Don Stuttgard's parents, too—were ashamed of . . . you know, the pregnancy, from the start. So Gabby came to live with us."

"You said you bailed her out plenty of times," Trapp said.

"Yes, Eustacia, but if you don't know about the biggest bailout we ever did, I bet you've guessed most of it."

"You kept her baby?" Trapp said. Her grandparents nodded.

"We adopted her—Nana Q. After all, she was already our niece. And she certainly made the loss of Rennie a little bit easier to bear—she darn near saved us. And she kept us right perky, even when we learned we wouldn't be able to have more children."

"You mean it was a secret from *everyone*?" Trapp asked.

"Only from Nana," Grandpa said. "Don Stuttgard knew, but all those years ago he probably felt as if it was more Gabby's secret—not his. Other folk just accepted the arrangement, but they didn't talk about it the way people do now."

"Gabby's parents never mentioned it," Grandma added. "Just never said a word while they were alive. She finally went away to school in New York, paid for some by herself, and the rest on family money. She stayed there. Bought a home when the market was soft. Then, a few years back, she started coming here each summer, to do her work on the farm. By then, what had happened, oh, two generations ago didn't much figure into anybody's business."

"Didn't she care about the baby?" Trapp asked. "Didn't she want to know about her own daughter?"

"We kept in touch with her, but Eustacia, honey," Grandma added, "it was a different time. She thought it was best for Nana Q if she grew up thinking we were her family. She was honor-bound to that baby never to breathe a word. And she had her work."

"What kind of work?" Trapp asked.

"Oh, Eustacia," Grandma said, "don't you ever run out of questions?"

Trapp shook her head, and then felt weary.

"Okay," Grandpa said. "That's enough for tonight. All these old memories floating around like ghosts. Hope we can sleep."

"But there's one thing," Trapp asked.

"What, honey?" Grandma said, concerned again.

"I *am* connected to you. I mean, we are still relatives, aren't we?"

Grandma stood up and wrapped Trapp in her soft embrace. "We would be family if you were a baby I'd found on my doorstep. We would be family if you had blown in on a stiff wind from the north. We would be family, Eustacia, if I'd walked into a roomful of babies and had only been allowed to pick out one. I'd have snatched you up the day you were born, and I'd like to see anyone take you away from me now. And that, no matter how many of us are born and live and die in this family, will never change."

(Pause.
A deep breath)

That was not all.

It was only the beginning for many more questions, much more explanation. Unresolved matters. Decisions.

Still, Trapp's sleep had been deep, with no stomachache to disturb her, and she had a comforting sensation, on waking, that she had breathed sweet, clear air all night long. They had made it to bed after the long talk. Grandma had held her as she'd fallen asleep, and Grandpa, still teary-eyed, had kissed her twice.

Rennie. A relative she never knew she had was her real great-grandfather. His laugh, frozen in the photograph, was haunting as if she had really heard it. She imagined that it was a friendly laugh, almost like Grandpa Hatfield's but younger, sprier, faster.

And Cleaver—he was some kind of cousin. Gabby was

her great-grandmother. There was a whole new parade of family relations to go through again.

Maybe she was growing up too fast, knowing too many things at once. People grew up in a place and spent a lifetime with someone, and put up one Christmas tree after another, then were expected to leave everything behind like so many shirts, or hats, or boots.

She just might have sense enough to put up with leaving one home for another, but great-grandparents and family names? Perhaps now New York was the only place for her, to start over again, for how could she claim any part of her old life as her own? She was angry that grown-ups could be so indifferent with information and events that mattered to her. Deciding, *for* her, whether fifty years ago or a few months ago, that something as crucial as a baby being adopted could be withheld from her, that actually moving to a new city was as easy as saying so.

She knew that moving away was her best revenge. Now she was ready to leave, ready to go on, and all by the path of a ball through a barn wall, and a photograph she had spotted in the Stuttgards' house while recovering from puking.

Accidents. Without some haphazard discoveries, she still wouldn't know about Nana Q. Was this how earth-shattering knowledge came to people? Being in a place at a particular moment to see the signs? What if she hadn't noticed?

Blindness or truth, Trapp decided, Gabby was a stranger, and Cleaver was a boy she had just met, who had become a friend—or perhaps the brother type she only *wished* Sam would be. She couldn't manufacture family feelings for either of them, just because of what had happened so many years before.

And she was mad at Gabby—for having a baby, then leaving it for reasons that Trapp couldn't even begin to understand. She could have found a way to raise it if she had really wanted to. That was it. Trapp was angry on behalf of that baby, which had become her Nana Q.

A deep path on the pine planks leading from her bed to the door showed the wear of all the people who had gotten up before her, over all the years the farmhouse had stood. The bed had been placed by the window forever, it seemed, and now, as she stood up, she didn't feel like herself, exactly, but as if she were someone doomed or blessed to travel that path again, without any choosing of her own.

It all had to do with other people's choices—Rennie's and Gabby's, and then her great-grandparents'. Everything they had done had led her to this wakeful moment, of knowing somehow that she almost had two families: the ones she had always known, and the ones who had descended on her the night before.

"Come on!" Cleaver—another Cleaver, who looked exactly the same as the one she knew—said from the bottom of the staircase. "We've got to get some ball practice!"

Trapp, in her nightgown, looked down at his upturned face, wondering that he was suddenly there, with his odd, angular body and near-radiant enthusiasm for the task ahead.

Did she feel affectionate toward him because they were

related? Or because from that first day, when he had fallen into step next to her, she had appreciated that he was someone who knew how to seize what was ahead while she was one who hung back, waiting for the prod?

"Gabby's here," he said. "She and your great-grand-mother are drinking coffee in the kitchen. They'll be done soon. Let's go!"

"Okay!" she found herself calling back. She knew that, in spite or because of the events of the previous night, she was ready to start the day. "Just a sec while I get dressed." Trapp backed up, grabbed her overalls off the back of the door, and pulled her nightgown off and a T-shirt on in one smooth move. She was glad that she wouldn't have to face Grandma Hatfield yet, that she didn't have to look in Gabby's eyes and find out if she knew what Trapp knew.

With ball and mitt in hand, she burst out the front door.

In which there is an initial explanation, but much remains murky, and a feeling lingers that there is still much to be answered for, and the gap between children's questions and adults' explanations becomes clearly unbridgeable

T rapp started to run after Cleaver, energetic despite the few hours of sleep. And suddenly Gabby was in Trapp's path.

Why, it almost seemed like a habit: that Gabby could appear before her at will, even if she was the last person on earth Trapp wanted to meet.

"Morning," Trapp said, mechanically. Years of good manners around ancient adults could not be suppressed.

"Hello to you, too," Gabby answered. "Can I walk with you for a bit?" Gabby was straight and tall for an old woman, but her delicacy was apparent in her long, bird-like fingers and hesitant step.

Trapp nodded without speaking.

"Your great-grandmother and I have been talking," Gabby said. "I always think of her as being wiser than I

118

am, because of ten short years between us. Can you imagine?"

Trapp could imagine—she saw how much older her Grandma Hatfield seemed than Gabby.

"I told her," Gabby said into Trapp's silence, "that I thought I might be able to help with some old secrets that have tumbled out from the mothballs—to air them out before the mold did some real harm."

Trapp looked at Gabby, and then back at the path. She did not want to talk, and she did not want to listen. She wanted to be left alone, to sit still and puzzle through the "secrets" all by herself. She did not want to have an adult—yet another adult—telling her what to do and what to think; it wasn't that she was mad but that she no longer liked the way everyone else was handling her life. Having a baby and then leaving it behind, uprooting her from the only home she had ever known, and now knew wasn't even hers—Gabby *or* her parents, hadn't they done enough?

"She reminded me of my work," Gabby continued. "Of the reason I went away, and the reason I came back."

"I don't know why you're talking to me like this," Trapp protested. "I'm sorry, but I don't really think I want to talk about anything like that."

Gabby's eyes seemed to turn kind. "Trapp," the elderly woman said. "I want you to know that I won't be around much longer." She paused, and waited for Trapp to question her, but Trapp would not.

"I don't mean in the way that your grandparents won't be around much longer—they'll outlive all of us, and they'll certainly outlive me. It's a private thing for me. Cleveland knows—only because we're close, and because he asked a lot of questions, and I couldn't lie. But it's one of the reasons he's so protective of me. And now you know, too."

All along, it had been *her*, her real great-grandmother: the one Trapp should have been worried about—had she known the truth. Not the Hatfields—it was true, they looked as if they would be around for always. She was right to be sad, she had reasons to be sad, and as if by some unearthly bamboozle—as Grandpa Hatfield would say—she had known it all along.

"Now I have to listen," Trapp said finally, softly. "But I do not like it that you said that. It's not really nice, and it's not really fair."

Gabby chuckled, low in her chest, and said, "Cleveland would say it's very unsporting. He'd be right. You're right. But listen, please. Since I have you here, with me, for once."

Trapp stopped walking, faced Gabby, and nodded again.

Gabby's gaze nearly drilled Trapp into the ground, forcing her to look away from the older woman, to turn her body slightly around and put at least a bony shoulder between them.

Gabby seemed to be counting Trapp's freckles, or concentrating on the number of eyelashes she had on each eyelid, or maybe just making sure her eyebrows were the same shape. It made Trapp wish for a mask to stop feeling so exposed. No adult had examined Trapp so closely, really planting her with that look, rooting her to the ground.

Trapp couldn't leave without appearing rude. But if Gabby were her own age, Trapp would seriously consider challenging her to a ball-throwing match, or suggesting a brisk walk—anything, to stop the scrutiny. But she felt like a criminal, running away from Gabby's eyes, and hated feeling as if she should hide, when she had done nothing wrong.

Trapp drew herself up, and turned toward the elderly woman, and stared right back. Lines fanned out like the spokes of two crazy wheels around Gabby's eyes. Her eyebrows looked like two flat minus signs over her eyes, and her mouth, pursed, made something like a plus sign. She had cheeks with high tanned planes, a chin pointed like a right angle, a neck of weathered flesh.

And as Trapp watched Gabby watching her, discomfort fell away. Fond curiosity was behind Gabby's face; not lively, puppy-like, exclamation-point curiosity like Cleaver's, but a slow, serious, melting interest that unrolled steadily like a clock's steady tick.

Only the merest of seconds had passed since she had first faced Gabby, but Trapp felt she wasn't being dismissed, and it both pleased and surprised her.

"You think I went away and forgot everyone and everything, don't you?" Gabby began. "But Nana Q and Rennie were the reasons for my life's work—out of grief I threw myself into it, and every minute I spent working was in the name of trying to make sense of my loss—two losses, really."

"What work?" Trapp asked.

"Botany," Gabby said. "You know what that is, I'm sure. Just as I know a lot about you, Trapp.

"Years and years of separating flower strains, of identifying genetic makeups, of trying to create perfect blooms," she said. "It sounds a bit lofty, but it's not. Fine. But I've finally had to stop. It had to happen sometime. My eyes are too tired for a microscope, and my hands are too shaky for the slides."

Trapp ducked her head.

"It's all right," Gabby said, "you don't have to understand. But let me tell you this: I tried to control all the factors, and I may have succeeded somewhat. But the most perfect flowers were always the ones outside the lab, the ones that I hadn't tampered with, the random pollen path, the accidents. Forgive me . . . my indulgence; I have to say so much in a little time. I may look like another stuffy old adult. I can only do my best."

Gabby was going on and on, as if she had just discovered words under a rock. "I don't expect you to easily forget all that has been done to you without your knowledge," she said to Trapp, breathing hard between her words. "A botanist can learn about things, and know about them, and think about them. But not interfere, not really, that's what I know now. There is nature and then there is something called nurture. I can't pretend to know the answers, but there is much to be said for doing my best, for working with what I had—" Gabby stopped abruptly. She had an empty look on her face. "Nature's always one step ahead, that's all."

Trapp pushed her ball into her mitt, and ground it

around. "I wondered," she finally said, without looking Gabby in the eye, "why you couldn't come up with a way to stay here."

Gabby sighed, shook her head in irritation, and replied, "I don't know why I am making myself answerable to a slip of a girl who doesn't know just how much the world has changed in fifty years. Except in all that time, I've never really had to answer to anyone else. And"—she jabbed out her words with short, quick gasps—"we are related.

"I will tell you this. That you figured it out—I am delighted. Purely delighted, in a way that only the dying know."

Trapp shuddered—she couldn't help it, but didn't drop her eyes. And she realized that Gabby always seemed out of place; she wasn't like anyone else Trapp had ever talked to, or ever met.

"After Rennie, I couldn't stay here, and live by what— by faith alone?" Gabby asked. "I saw a whole world out there of questions and, best of all, where nothing was acceptable until it was justified and proven to be true— *proven*, do you hear?" Trapp nodded.

Gabby stared at the ground where they were standing, and her face broke into a grin. She leaned over, and held up a pea pod wayward from the compost pile, pushed it at Trapp triumphantly. "Do you know how much more there is to know about corn and peas—these peas and corn that all of us have spent endless summers shelling and cooking and freezing?" She shook her head, and spoke to herself. "Corn, and its descendants, and its ancestors, and its chromosomes, unto the Middle Ages and before the first Christmas and even before the plow was ever heard of?"

Trapp was uncomfortable; it was as if a madwoman were confronting her—Gabby's voice was high, and she seemed to shriek many of her words. Out of the "Blah, blah, blah, blah, blah, blah, blah, blah, blah, blah, blah, blah, blah, blah, blah, blah, blah, blah," Trapp understood all of it to mean that she—Trapp—was supposed to "get" stuff about agriculture and creation and the science of corn, and all of it was supposed to explain *why* Gabby had to move or something and *how* Trapp had a—practically a new identity. She would tell her parents about that, yes, and maybe have a good laugh—about the idea of everybody changing their names—or maybe the way they looked—every time they exchanged one address for another. She would see how they liked *that*.

Gabby seemed to sense Trapp's confusion and discomfort, and gave herself a little shake.

"I'll just say this," she told Trapp. "In *my* experience, just to go away and discover how much there is to know made returning here that much easier—if I thought I was living a quiet dull life here, I was wrong, because there are miracles all around, all day long, and I don't mean God-sent ones."

"I don't really understand anything you said or what you're telling me," Trapp said. "Just say something I can understand."

Gabby sighed once and looked around the farm. "I knew that the baby belonged here, just as I never had.

And I was right. Nana Q loved the Hatfields, and then there was your mother, who loved the farm so, and now you. You saw the meadow," she stated flatly. Trapp nodded. "It's thriving. Because any plant that doesn't belong here either dies out or adapts.

"*I* couldn't adapt, and I couldn't just die," Gabby said, crying. "So I left."

Trapp was crying herself, as it dawned on her that Gabby had lost Nana Q last year, too. Maybe Gabby was trying to say to her that she had to leave the farmlands, but she left the baby behind so that part of her would grow up and appreciate what she never had been able to love. As if she did something, without really knowing why, and figured it out years later.

Trapp knew then that no explanation would ever be enough to make her understand, but she was as sorry for Gabby as she was for herself. "I think I really do see, maybe."

Gabby's face cleared. "And what do you think?" she asked. "Should we, all these years later, spell everything out to everyone?" Was there any reason her parents *had* to know what she knew? It was possible they hadn't known, but she might have the duty to tell. Was it a secret kept from her, or that she was keeping?

"*No* one knows?" Trapp said, as puzzled as she had been the night before.

"I don't see a sign of it," answered Gabby. "If they do, and aren't saying anything, I haven't told them, and if they don't, I'm not going to be the one to tell them. Not now. Not at this late hour."

Didn't people have a right to know where they came from, who their relatives were? Trapp remembered the path from her bed to the door, and then the musty ancestors in her grandma's parlor, and up ahead, the green, shimmering leaves of the poplars planted by those who had first farmed the fields of corn.

Gabby was silent then. "I'm too old," she said quietly, after a pause. "Too old to want to take on the past, even if it is all I have left."

"I don't know if my mother should know or not," Trapp said. "I can't say, just now. But I can't pretend"— Trapp hesitated—"pretend I know you, or like you, as anything but a friend of my great—of the Hatfields." Trapp hesitated again. "I mean, not yet."

"I know."

"I can't feel—anything. I mean, the way I feel about my great-grandparents." She repeated "great-grandparents" under her breath. It still felt right.

She faced Gabby. "That has to be okay. Okay?"

Gabby stuck out one hand. Trapp took it and gave it a shake. It was enough, she thought.

"I have to go back to the house," Gabby said suddenly. "Nature calls. Someone my age should never drink that much coffee without being prepared to slosh a little." She turned to leave. "It's too much coffee for one day, *I'd* say. For anyone, even you. You probably don't like it anyway. Kids shouldn't be made to drink it. Not if they don't have to." She was away without another word.

Cleaver approached her then, his face curious. "I have

to say, I've never seen Gabby say that much to anyone," he told her. "What was all that about?"

"Nothing, um, Kansas City, Kansas," she said to him. She was clumsy, but she wanted to distract him. He'd had the grace to stay out of earshot while she and Gabby talked. She hoped he wouldn't ask more questions, or make any remarks.

His only reply was sharp, but held a trace of good humor. "Have it your way, New York, New York."

Some key conversations before the big windup

In the first weeks of August, Trapp tried to find out from Grandpa and Grandma which secrets were improper to talk about, and which were permitted. Nana Q's adoption gnawed at her.

Grandma Hatfield was the first to catch on. "Eustacia, there are secrets, and then there are secrets," Grandma said. She sat by the kitchen table while Trapp dried the last of the heavy pots. "If you know how to look at things, why then, a secret is just something you've noticed but haven't yet put words to."

"What do you mean?" asked Trapp. She put a still-greasy frying pan back in the sink. If Grandma found it, she would be sure to ban Trapp from the kitchen. "You're supposed to talk about secrets, that's what everyone says."

"Bad secrets, that's true. Good secrets, maybe not. But

the kind of secret I mean, is . . . well, see here. Do you know how I bake bread—do you know my recipe?"

"No," Trapp replied. "You don't have it written down anywhere."

"No, I don't, but if you asked me, I'd tell you. It's not a secret—we just don't bring it up. And someone with a piece of warm bread in the hand doesn't much think about the recipe. The flavor's the thing—real and nourishing. If you were a gourmet cook, you could probably figure out how much white flour, how much whole wheat, how much molasses and salt I put into it, because you'd know how to look at a loaf of bread, and taste it, and figure it out."

"Grandma!" Trapp yelled. She was puzzled. "But what's that got to do with *Gabby*?" she asked.

Grandma Hatfield pulled a chair away from the table for Trapp to sit down, then took one of her hands, and patted it, sandwich-like, between her own.

"I know you can't put your finger on it," she said. "Neither can I. Well now, take those wildflowers. Say that some seeds from the dried pods in Gabby's meadow crossed over this way, and took root in our yard. Most people would pass those flowers, if they bloomed, and say, 'How nice.' But an expert maybe, or someone who knew how to look at that flower, would say, 'Look how a big old wind brought some of Gabby's species all the way over here.' "

"Grandma—do you mean that just because no one's asking about something doesn't make it a secret?"

"Well, you tell me. Is that a secret, honey? Is it something people are deliberately *not* talking about or hiding? Or is it just a part of the picture and if people ask, why, we'd tell 'em?"

"Now, why can't grownups speak plain, Grandma?" Trapp said. "I'm trying to understand. Gabby's secret wasn't really a secret but just something no one ever talked about?"

"Yes," Grandma told her. "That's all there is. Now listen some more. I told you about the gourmet cook, and about the flower expert—the way I see it, you're sort of a family expert. While Sam or Maggie, bless 'em both, are chattering away, or running around getting into trouble, you're the type who sits there taking in things no one else notices, and stirring it around in that head of yours until you come up with real ideas. And trouble."

Trapp said, "My mother always accuses me of moping around, and brooding all the time—"

"I know, I know," Grandma interrupted. She tried to dismiss the sentence with a squeeze of Trapp's hands. "And spending too much time by yourself—I've heard all about that from your mother; bless her heart, she has nothing but good intentions. But the way you tussle through things till you've figured them out is real special, and if you need to be alone to do it, well, why not? The person who's her own best company will never be lonely—that's how these old bones feel about that situation."

Trapp grinned down at her lap, pleased. Then she said, as if to herself, "So everyone knew why Gabby ran off, but it was the kind of thing people didn't talk about—a private sort of thing. And even though you weren't pregnant, your neighbors just accepted that Nana Q was yours."

"That's right—and you're right about the privacy. People around here know each other a little too well, so the least we can all do is know what's gossip for the coffeepot and what're personal feelings, not to be bruised by small talk."

"And now," Trapp continued, "all those years later, when my own mother came along, people weren't really keeping a secret, were they? It was just someone's old news that no longer mattered?"

Grandma stood up. "Honey, I just told you. That's all there is. All the folks involved were either dead or past caring about such things. I don't know if you've noticed, but the Stuttgards and the Hatfields are just about the oldest relics around here—Grandpa and I have outlived or outstayed the people we knew as young marrieds."

"Except Don and Gabby."

"Yes, but they're more like a younger brother and sister to us—even though to you we're all just a bunch of old geezers."

"No, I understand," Trapp said. "I just have to try to think about all this."

"Of course you do, honey. You have to look at every door and window and chimney pipe," Grandma Hatfield said, "and find your own way in—or out. Don't ever forget how you got your nickname, Eustacia."

Trapp grinned again, this time right at Grandma. "And you're not an old geezer," she protested, knowing that her words were late. "But you are old."

"I know," Grandma said as she pushed herself away from the table. "And you will be, too, someday. I just hope when that day comes, you have a great-granddaughter as nice as mine to keep you company."

"About this moving thing," Cleaver said as he sat on the tree stump just outside the kitchen. He was carving vegetables into thick lumps for pickling. "You never talk about it. You never say anything. How can you take it? I'd be scared to death."

"You have green pea gunk stuck between your teeth," Trapp answered. She grinned over her bowl of shelled peas as he flushed, and popped one into her own mouth.

Cleaver recovered quickly. He wiped his teeth with one finger and then asked, "Is that your way of avoiding an answer?"

She pulled down the string of the pea shell, like a long smooth zipper, fascinated as always that it didn't break before it came off cleanly at the bottom. Then she slightly pinched the shell, and it opened neatly, the peas falling lightly into the bowl. The first peas into the metal bowl were like rain on a tin roof, but now they fell soundlessly. Trapp and Cleaver had finally eaten their fill, and the bowls were nearly ready to go inside to the kitchen, for the peas to be emptied onto cookie sheets and frozen, then stored in bags for the winter. Then she would help Cleaver finish the pickling vegetables.

The first harvest—of sweet corn—would begin in a couple of weeks, and Trapp couldn't remember how her grandparents would manage it, how they had managed it all these years—they said that Rakes always brought in crews, but not every field could be harvested at the same time, and bad weather could set the process back days. Trapp knew that she would probably pick the entire kitchen garden by herself, but she didn't mind.

She raised her head, meeting Cleaver's look, which had not let up since he had asked his question.

"I suppose some of this canning stuff will travel," Cleaver said.

"I suppose," she answered. Trapp knew that if Grandma had her way, her family's new pantry would be stocked for many winters.

"Whole armies, you know, march on their stomachs," Cleaver continued for good measure.

"I'm not good at making friends," she finally said. "And I liked living in—in—where we lived. But all that's changed now." Trapp put her head down again. She no longer believed that she could stay behind. She was half-way there. Her father had told her New York was a city of people who had come from other places. Now she figured it was a city for people who didn't belong anywhere else—and that suited her perfectly.

Cleaver chose to ignore her second sentence. "You sure made friends around here fast enough," he said. "That was easy. And you can always come visit. Me, I mean. We're practically family."

Trapp was startled and stared at him. "You know, our

133

great-grandparents being such old friends, and every-thing," he added hastily. "Jeez, what are you looking at?"

Trapp almost laughed, but instead just shook her head. If she decided not to tell about Nana Q, she would have to get used to carrying around that baggage. Maybe it would be like the sap that her great-grandfather never tapped from the sugar maples in the lane. It would run freely, bothering no one, hers to hold on to.

Cleaver was right. She could visit. It wasn't as if she were moving away forever. She always made it seem as if she were going to another planet. But there were still all those unknowns, new smells, new tastes, new faces, that she knew she was afraid of.

"I'm not really good at selling myself—isn't that what you're supposed to do in that part of the world?" she finally admitted. "I'm just afraid. Of everything. But I think I'm not worried about being afraid anymore. Maybe my parents have to be savvy, but *I* don't. I'll just have to figure everything out once I get there."

"Good," Cleaver said. "Because I want to be savvy enough to come visit you any time of the year, whether Gabby is there or not. I figured that since you have to go through an entire move, the least I can do is to continue to be more actively interested in athletics. So I need you to coach me."

"The way Rakes has coached us on the harvest plans this summer? It's chilly," Trapp said, surprised, as the sun went under a cloud. The kitchen yard was hot, even in the shade, but the wind shifted, and she saw bumps rise on her legs.

"It may be early, but fall's in the air," Grandma Hatfield said from the screen door. She shuffled outside and picked up the bowls, nodding with satisfaction. "Shells, stems, peels, and seeds go in the compost pile," she reminded them. "They'll start wasting before we even get these put up."

"I know, I know," Trapp said. "Everything is either growing or rotting on a farm."

"People, too," Grandma said. "That's the way it is the world over."

"That's depressing," Cleaver said. He stood up and threw a baseball into the air, catching it neatly in his mitt.

"No," Trapp said. "It's not."

Grandpa was striding up the lane, sorting through envelopes and fliers he had gathered from the mailbox. "Something for Trapp," he called. "From your parents."

"Well, at last," Grandma said. "You sure have a stretched neck waiting for that letter, honey."

Trapp ran to meet Grandpa. He handed her the yellow envelope that held her mother's matching stationery, but she didn't open it at once.

Her brother Sam always said, "The best news comes over the telephone," so she was disappointed to get the letter. Now that she had resigned herself to moving, she was a little anxious to get under way. If she was going home to the new house, she was sure they would have phoned to tell her. The last phone call had been all about a show they had seen; but they still hadn't known when they were moving.

"Here," she said, handing the letter to her grandmother.

"You open it. Set another place at the table—I'll be here until Christmas."

"No you won't," Grandma said. Her eyes scanned the first sheet. "No, you'll be back for Thanksgiving—your mother already wrote me about that. But they're coming next week." At her words, Cleaver turned away, suddenly busy with his mitt.

Grandpa sat down next to Trapp on the kitchen-door porch step with a sigh. "So we're losing you," he said. "Hate to admit it, Trapp, but I was thinking you'd have to take charge of things around here for the harvest, even at the risk of breaking child labor laws. Now maybe we'll just dutch the darn harvest after all."

"Grandpa! Skip harvest?" Trapp cried. She was pretty sure he was teasing. She held out her hand for the letter. Her grandmother gave it to her with a smile.

"Bad luck to stop the cycle. But, maybe," he said. She couldn't tell if he was joking.

For a few days, Trapp and her great-grandmother had either been outside, cutting the vegetable garden into pickle-sized pieces, or inside, peeling and quartering to-matoes for sauce or sterilizing jars in large pans over the stove and sealing them, full and glistening, with a satis-fying whoosh of air. Even if her parents did come before the major canning events of the season, at least the cellar was starting to look normal again, with jams, pickles, and sauces beginning to line the walls like perfectly cut stones.

The summer sun was behind the trees, throwing long shadows over the fields in the distance. Trapp was using a few free moments on the porch step, kneading her mitt with a thumb. The leather was perfectly oiled, smooth as marble, pliable as cloth. She valued it even more after watching Cleaver spend much of the past few weeks breaking in his brand-new, factory-stiff glove. She had given him her oil, and he had applied it by pouring it over the mitt like syrup over pancakes. It made her smile, and dimly she realized that her great-grandmother was calling to her from the kitchen.

"Grandma?" she answered. "I wasn't listening."

"That's all right, honey," Grandma said, entering the porch. "I bet your move and your new school are nagging at you again."

Trapp shrugged. "I guess." At least the word "move" no longer marched through her brain in large capital letters.

"Here you are, almost at the end of this long episode, when you're supposed to be relieved and perky and full of pomp and circumstance as you speedily move on to the next thing," Grandma said, amused. "Instead you're all anticlimax-tic and saggy like your old grandmother."

Trapp smiled but didn't speak. Grandma put a bowl in her lap, and they both began to sort herbs from a long oval basket—some to dry, some to snip up and put into vinegar. It was a long, satisfying stretch, requiring little thought, and Trapp felt herself returning to that now familiar ache that had filled almost every moment ever since she had turned twelve and especially in the weeks after she heard about the move.

Some odd longing lodged in her gut, and she knew it

was there, and wanted to do something to it, or around it, but the way it lingered on, filling her with need she didn't understand, made it hard to breathe. All the answers, all the questions . . .

She heaved a deep breath, a huge gratifying one that perked her up a bit and cleared her head.

"You've been mighty quiet out here, Eustacia," Grandma said. The sigh seemed to have dislodged her from her reverie, too. "Just what are you all dreamy-eyed about?"

It took Trapp a moment to remember what she had been thinking about—it wasn't a thing, or a place, exactly. "I don't know, Grandma," she replied. "Sort of nothing, I guess."

"Oh, shucks, honey," Grandma said, not looking up from her task. "You got me wound up here, about being your age, and I can't remember sights and people's faces anymore, but I sure know that sigh. It comes from a feeling, I suppose, like looking at a gadfly on sticky paper—it was annoying when it was buzzing around, but it just hurts to see it stuck there, so still."

Trapp didn't answer—Grandma didn't seem to expect her to say anything. Grandma continued talking. "Those feelings, honey—hold on to them. The next few years you're just going to take it all in with every breath, and a lot of it's going to hurt—right here"—she pointed to the center of her chest—"to the left of your heart or even sometimes in your tummy. Boys don't get it, but we do. It's awful, just awful, but when it goes away—when you settle down and quit considering every tiny thing, from the way you tie your shoe to determining the exact shade you blush in front of boys—why, that's worse." She seemed no longer aware of the rosemary in her hands, and looked out over the fields. Her voice became soft, and still.

"I used to sit on this porch, when I was first married, and in those days the air was so clear I think you could see just about all the way to Ames," she said. "Now there's a sort of a haze out that way, hanging over the crops even when the skies are bluest, but I don't know if that's me, or the air, or my memory—which is bust. I used to sit here, shelling peas, or shucking corn, and I'd tell myself, 'Eustacia, just get over it, just forget it.' "

"Forget what?" Trapp asked, afraid to interrupt, but wondering what Grandma meant.

"Well, that's just it—I don't know," Grandma told her.

"Don't know now, or didn't know then?"

"Then, or now. I just had this tug, this yank, that seemed to be saying I should—don't laugh at your old grandma—walk through the grass without my shoes in the early morning dew, sort of, well, do things. Really do them. And notice them while I was doing them, and remember them when I was done."

"Sort of all dancy inside," Trapp said.

"That's it, honey," Grandma said, looking right at Trapp. "I felt all dancy inside, and I wanted to spin and twirl up and down that lane of sugar maples till I fell over breathless." She bent her head over her bowl, and to Trapp, for a moment, it was like looking at a young girl, ducking behind a sheath of hair in shyness. And then the image was gone, because Grandma's hair was rolled back into a soft knot and anchored snugly with pins so that she couldn't hide behind it.

"What did you do?"

"Well, I am one hundred percent positive that I just kept shucking the corn or shelling those peas, and that the feeling passed. But when it left me—and I think now, I think this now and I didn't know it then—it just *took* something from me, and I would dearly love, Eustacia, another chance to feel that way again."

It felt like the last time Trapp would pinch herb petals or shell peas in her whole life, she thought. It made her look, for the first time, at her own young hands, to watch this ritual that might never take place again.

"And you can't hurry over it, Eustacia," Grandma told her, continuing, "or rush past it, or tumble through it— darn, look at this old lady here, going on and on about nothing—Eustacia, honey, you just got to allow yourself a place to breathe, all your own, and take the ache with the pure goodness of it. Because listen to the person sitting next to you here, still shelling peas for heaven's sake: put your hands around it—you can't, you know—but try, try to put your arms around it and hold it in place. And I think maybe there's a little piece of joy in trying."

Why not get the whole family in on it? But without the sorrowful mood that plagued the first few episodes

Trapp heard Grandpa shuffle toward the porch. The afternoon had passed in a sequence of half-hearted sunlight filtered through wispy, passing clouds. He had finished his day as punctually as the period at the end of a sentence and sat down on the top step with a sigh, like a sack of grain settling into itself with a puff of dust.

"If Rakes's workers don't show up soon, you and I are going to have to go get that crop of sweet corn one ear at a time until the day you leave," he said to Trapp. "And your grandma, too."

"When did he say they'd be here?" Grandma asked. "You know better'n to doubt Rakes's word."

"I swear, I'll leave Rakes in charge around here through eternity if he gets us that help in time—he has been in charge, anyway," Grandpa Hatfield replied. "He says they're taking care of their own harvest plans—can't blame 'em—but timing will be pretty tight."

"But they're supposed to help you," Trapp pointed out.

"That's how you and I see it," Grandpa told her, "but these folk have to stay where the work is when the work is there, and go where the work is when the work is not."

"A riddle, sounds like," Grandma said.

"No, I get it," Trapp said. "So they can't just quit to get here."

"Not really," Grandpa said. "Because even if they up and left their own land to get here, I could be hit by a hailstorm while they're on the road. And they'd be up here for nothing."

"Praise be," Grandma said, "don't deal any disasters on us. Don't mind him, Eustacia honey, that's just about what he says every year around this time. It's part of the ritual."

"It will be a disaster if we don't get that crop in," Grandpa said. "Only thing sorrier is the man who couldn't keep his rows straight. Now, if we'd decided not to plant at all, that would be one thing. But we invested time, money, labor. For the hundredth year in a row—so it feels like—we did everything we're supposed to and then stood back and hoped. Near to break my heart to go out this way."

"Go out? What's 'this way'?" Trapp asked.

"Like a darned old feather duster," Grandpa said. "Letting the corn rot on the stalk, until it turns to compost in its own field. It would be a sin."

"But some things grow by themselves," Trapp pointed out, remembering Gabby's meadow.

142

"True, it's true," he agreed. "Gotta be natural about these things, though. Corn doesn't grow that way—can't reproduce unaided. Corn needs people—people to tend it." He shook his head. "Hell!"

"Ralph!" Grandma said, shocked.

"What?" Trapp asked. She tried to make herself clear. "Why did you say 'hell'?"

"Because all these years I thought I was growing corn," Grandpa said. "And I just figured out that the corn's been growing *me*."

"Company! Yikes, you have company," Cleaver screamed from the lane. His long legs looked like bent, blurred extensions of the bike pedals, moving like smooth levers as he slowed down and coasted to a stop in front of them. "Workers on the way to your house. Experienced."

He leaped off the bike by bringing one leg over the seat, allowing the bike to crash behind him as he landed lightly and strode to the porch. "Their car—a Lincoln, looks like—gave out on our road. Maybe they just ran out of gasohol or something—so Don is bringing them over."

"That's blessed news," Grandma said, fanning herself with a piece of the mail. "That's certainly a relief."

"How many of them are there?" Grandpa asked Cleaver. "Are these Rakes's people?"

"No, I don't think they're with Rakes," Cleaver replied. "There's, um, four of them, so far." He winked at Trapp the way her grandfather usually did. "Just four. But they look like good hard workers."

143

Grandpa took his cap off, wiped his sweaty forehead with the back of his hand, and fluffed his damp white hair with his fingers. "I don't know," he said. "Better than nothing, but we'd started with six workers last year. Golly damn! In the four-square states of Iowa, South Dakota, Nebraska, and Minnesota—you'd think I could find enough help, wouldn't you?"

"A couple of them are kind of puny," Cleaver said hurriedly, heading off more of Grandpa's curses. "But they look willing. Really willing."

Trapp watched Cleaver's face carefully, trying to see if the mischief in it was for the good or the bad. "I don't know if you'll get a full day's work out of them for your wages." He avoided Trapp's eyes and did two cartwheels on the lawn. He came full circle and was upright again; then he looked at them and grinned.

Trapp took a deep breath. Cleaver was up to something, but it was good. She was ready for something good to happen. It would be all right.

Grandpa's hair had dried in the breeze. He stared out at the road. "Well, I don't guess we have much choice," he said. Trapp saw that his blue eyes were tearier than usual as he peered in the direction of Don's coughing, catching truck engine. They all heard it before they saw it, and then spotted the dust kicked up around the tops of the sugar maples, marking the truck's speed. Just as the vehicle began to emerge from the lane of trees, it chugged twice and came to a dead, silent halt. The film of dust it had set up began to settle as people opened the doors of the truck—three from the front cab, and two off the back.

"Don said he'd help you guys," Cleaver said, into the silence. "He said he'd send over our workers, too, when he could."

Trapp watched him spin on his spindly legs, and followed his gaze. Don stood facing them, squat and round. "You folks need some laborers?" he called out. "These people say they came to help with the harvest. Say there'll be even more of 'em tomorrow, first convoy out of Mason City. Know 'em?"

Trapp slowly stood up, brushing the last of the thready tassels from her lap. Cleaver glanced back at her over one bony shoulder and nodded. She looked at him, and she was thinking, *Smile at him, he made a surprise out of this for you*, but later she wouldn't know whether a smile came out or not. The next few minutes passed slowly, carefully, as if the world had suddenly gone from a full-motion, full-color movie to a daguerreotype of images frozen in black, gray, white, and beige.

In a stillness so complete that she heard her own eyelids open and close, and seemed to hear, too, the gush of new tears that passed into Grandpa's eyes, Trapp saw events as if they were chronicled in a photo album. The people climbing out of Don's truck moved as if distantly, as if she was only mildly attached to them—as if they were photo-colored. A man dressed in overalls and a T-shirt, with wild, dust-covered hair, had a whitey-white grin that dazzled with snapshot clarity. His work boots ground the dirt beneath as he turned back to the truck to lift out a small girl. He held her in his arms while she wiped the grime of the road from her eyes; then he remained there with his legs slightly apart—defiant, proud, happy. The girl's legs wrapped around his back, her spine small and straight. She put one arm around his neck and with the other waved at Trapp.

These events might have happened long ago, with the field of corn behind the truck, almost in every photo in Grandpa's house. Only the people changed over time. She waved back and felt as silly as if she had waved at a photograph. The girl's smile mirrored her own. Yes, I recognize that grin; yes, I know this family. How are they related to me again?

"I'm a sucker for homecomings," Grandpa said quietly. "Can't seem to get enough of 'em lately. Gollee damn! They weren't gonna be here till tomorrow."

On the other side of the truck, Trapp's mother and Sam were dressed in overalls, and, Trapp noticed, almost the same height. Her mother had lines around her eyes and a mouth that almost said, "This is a woman who doesn't stop smiling; this is a woman accustomed to work." Sam looked at Trapp shyly, his head bent slightly down over his chest, his eyes peering out from a sheath of hair grown too long from his summer in the city.

I know these people, Trapp thought, smiling; I do. Familiarity washed over her and unfroze the time that stood between them. And the stillness was sucked out of the air, replaced instead with the calls of her mother and father, her brother and sister, as she ran toward them and tried to gather them all at once to her chest, like an armful of meadow flowers. She enclosed herself in their circle. At the beginning of the summer, she had tried to carry some unframed pictures of her relatives near her chest, just like now. They had felt cold, and shiny, and terribly, uncomfortably flat, like fall leaves, but not as warm and fragrant and scratchy and real. They had not hugged her back, but had slipped out of her hands and into her lap, and stared up at her, unmoving.

She felt four hearts beating close to her own, and more arms than she could count holding her, stroking her back, her head, and most of all the sighs—the sighing, welcoming noises they made as she once again entered the fold.

The powwow:
why green gelatin salad
is still revered in the heart
of the part of the country where a
handshake is as good as an ironclad
contract

A noisy caravan of station wagons and recreation ve-
hicles and stuffed-to-the-roof sedans, with uncles,
aunts, cousins, and a good many children, began
to arrive the next morning—in addition to Rakes's own
band of relations, who were as punctual as migratory
birds. Trapp wasn't sure who had put out the call to her
relatives—her father from Don's house, or her mother
from New York; all she knew was that for the first time
in her memory, the first harvest was turning into some
sort of patched-together gathering of kith and kin.

Trapp's father and Sam had slipped off to the machinery shed, where Rakes had already inspected the combine.
Parts had to be ordered before the big dent-corn harvest
at the end of the next month, but everything they needed
for the immediate work was ready.

Trapp was dawdling at the kitchen table with her

mother, Grandma Hatfield, and Maggie when the first cars began to honk greetings as they turned into the lane of sugar maples. The slam of car doors and Grandpa's rousing yelps from the front yard were exchanged like cannon fire.

"I was hoping we'd have a little time this morning for visiting," Trapp's mother said, looking at her fondly. "Now that my family's all in one place again, I feel a little too selfish to spend time with others."

"I know," Trapp said. "But you'll miss all of them when we move." The moment was near when Trapp knew she had to bring up Nana Q with her mother— that she would have to do it either while they were still at the farm, or not at all.

"Didn't miss anyone this summer," Maggie said, squirming in the chair. "Didn't care. Trapp, you want to see my lanyards? I made 'em in lizard colors."

Trapp shook her head.

"Honey, *I'd* like to look at your doo-buggies later on," Grandma said, plugging in the forty-cup coffee urn. "But first, you want to help me set out these rolls and apple cider? Folks are always hungry after a long drive."

Maggie stood up agreeably and took a platter of iced cinnamon buns from the counter.

"Grandma, they haven't traveled far," Trapp's mother chided. "They just used that as an excuse all summer long not to get out here. My, I don't know why. Even on the nicest days in New York, I couldn't get this place out of my head. Just couldn't wait to see you again."

"Folks have busy lives," Grandma said easily. "Can't

expect them to drive out to the middle of nowhere on a whim."

The screen door screeched open and Aunt Lily emerged and burst into the kitchen.

"Shirley!" she shrieked at Trapp's mother before they embraced. "I thought you'd cut more of a flash, sweetie. Living la-di-da in New York is supposed to make all of you into high-society so-phis-ti-cates."

"You know me," Trapp's mother replied, staring down at her worn jeans and plaid shirt with long frayed sleeves. "Dressing right for the occasion has always been one of my strong points."

Grandpa Hatfield came beaming into the kitchen, his cheeks flushed and eyes flashing. "Trapp, everyone's looking for you outside—heck, they act as if you were the one who's been away. Lily, you didn't even say hello! Rushing about, everyone's rushing about, disrupting the peace. Haven't seen so much excitement since the Iowa Shriners passed through Main Street a few years back." He shuffled over to his wife and craned over to kiss her on the neck. "We got plenty of company, Eustacia, and I'm kind of concerned there won't be enough food for them all," he said teasingly.

He winked at Trapp, but Grandma turned to him with uncharacteristic worry in her eyes. "I should have cracked those last few fryers," she said. "I knew there wouldn't be enough, even with the roast pig."

Aunt Lily hushed Grandma just as Trapp's mother interrupted. "Grandma, there's never been any shortage of food or drink in all the times our kinfolk got together—

150

why are you fretting so?" she asked. She spoke Grandma's language better than anyone.

"I haven't done this for ages," Grandma said anxiously. "I might have lost my touch. People might need more. Kids have grown and need extra nourishment. This—this getting-old business!" she burst out. "You just wait— you'll see why I worry." She angrily swiped at one eye, where tears had gathered.

Aunt Lily and Trapp's mother exchanged glances, while Grandpa made it right. "Now, now, 'Stacia," he murmured. "You just come out with me to see everyone —they want to hug *you*, not a platter of cupcakes. The girls here will take care of everything—if you've left them anything to do, that is."

With one arm around Grandma's shoulder and the other holding her arm, Grandpa led her out of the kitchen.

"It's Nana Q," Aunt Lily said in the pause after the two old people went outside.

"I know," Trapp's mother replied, her voice quavering slightly. "I was wondering when it would hit her."

It sank in, then, and Trapp was surprised at herself for making it through the entire summer, the first season of growing since Nana Q had died. It was the first full-scale family reunion since the funeral.

"They say you never expect to outlive your kids," Aunt Lily added. "It would have done for me to visit them this summer, wouldn't it? Especially with you away. But—but you get so busy, you know? And missing Nana Q the way we all do . . ." She was silent for a moment. "Oh, gee,

Shirley," she said suddenly. "Do you really have to move?"

"Can't imagine how hard it's been on them," Trapp's mother muttered, nodding. "I've only thought of myself, and leaving here." She pulled her shoulders back and looked at Aunt Lily. "Yes, we really do have to," she said, and launched into the list of reasons Trapp and Maggie had already heard, more than once.

Maggie shifted the platter she was holding to one hand and slipped her other into Trapp's as they listened to the older pair of sisters. Trapp shook away the notion that someday, somewhere, maybe she and Maggie would be having a conversation about *their* mother. Instead of making her sad, the notion was reassuring and funny—that even if individual lives didn't go on, Life did, with different generations having almost the same conversations. Grandpa Hatfield's parents wouldn't have expected to outlive Rennie, either, but they had, and the farm had gone on, without that younger brother and his gloom-busting grin.

Aunt Lily's daughters, Joy and Blissful Anne, pushed and shoved their way into the kitchen. They talked at the same time and hugged Trapp and Maggie, arguing over the ending of a joke their father had told in the car. It distracted Aunt Lily and Trapp's mother, and everyone began to pick up platters of breakfast food to take out to the colossal picnic table on the lawn.

Trapp made her way into the front yard. Summer was over. Her days at the farm were gone. Now she was just another relative visiting the Hatfields, crowding the old farmhouse with the others and making its usually quiet rooms ring with laughter. And Gabby, too, was just another relative.

At sundown, the pig was ready to pull out of the cooking pit. "Meat falling off the bone and Country Gentleman sweet corn," Trapp's father said. "There's nothing like it this side of heaven." He drew in the scent that mingled with foil-covered corn and new potatoes, buried in the ashes for the last hour.

"Aren't city folk more into cultured wheat than country corn?" Grandpa asked, poking the fire. Grandma brought out succotash and sheets of corn bread from the kitchen and handed them to Trapp.

"Wheat or corn, it's all good and ready for the grindstone," Trapp's father answered. "Food-processing technology is the only way to go these days. Excess and overproduction is a problem that won't go away—that and land erosion." Aunt Lily handed him her green gelatin salad, with grated carrots, chopped celery, and whole walnut halves mixed in and a thin layer of mayonnaise icing the top.

Rakes, who had been handling the fire with Grandpa's long, hefty pole, spoke his first words in hours. "It's true," he said. "The sod can take so much; it's like overpopulation—urban population in particular. When it looks like there are more people living than dead, there's some kind of imbalance in nature—and nature might just be angry." Then he fell silent, exiting the conversation faster than he had entered it. His straight face looked so still it was as if someone other than him had just been talking.

"Hell—maybe we're not meant to stay in one place," Grandpa said. "Looks like Old Man River here and me are a dying breed," pointing in Rakes's direction. "We're a country of roving-mad nomads, always on the move, and no place to rest."

"Or of globe-trotting pioneers," Trapp's father joked.

Rakes remained impassive. He stood up and walked quietly toward a group of children who were trying to hoist a cone-shaped tent.

"Oh, yes . . ." Grandpa said to Trapp's father. "What's the name of that new corporation you mentioned?"

"Millwright International."

"And what club—the Mercantile Club of . . . something . . . Hill or another. Of New York, that is?"

"Yes, Grandpa, but I'm still a member of your Agrarian Society, you know," Trapp's father said as he surveyed the table's bounty: other contributions of johnnycakes, bean casseroles in a mushroom-soup sauce with crunchy toppings of potato sticks, raw vegetable plates, macaroni— semolina tubes, Grandpa called them—salads full of green pepper and carrots, fresh asparagus buried in chowchow, plenty of chips, and vats of Kool-Aid for the kids, apple cider, soda pop, lemonade for the teenagers, and beer for the old and wise.

"How did you like the altitude in the Hancock building?" Cleaver asked enthusiastically, a big grin stamped on his face. "The one that's one hundred stories." He had been overjoyed to be included in the gathering. Don and Gabby had joined it at the end of the day, when the work at their own farm had come to a close for the night.

154

Trapp's father squatted by the fire and smiled. "Well, son, if that building were in New York, and I'm sorry to say it's not, my answer would be the same. I'm kind of used to it, you could say. Growing up out here, with open country as far as the eye could see, is like being on top of a silo, or—like being seated permanently in a belfry." He stopped momentarily, then said, pointing to the side of his head. "It's all up here."

Cleaver looked delighted by the answer, as if he had gotten more mileage from his question than he expected and not at all embarrassed by his mistake. Trapp kept listening quietly with arms folded.

"Do we have to listen to all this men's talk?" Maggie said, playfully swinging her legs.

"And boys'," Trapp added.

The two girls watched their mother pour some blue corn tortilla chips into a basket, slice up a polenta loaf, then push a large salad fork and spoon into a wooden bowl and toss a colorful batch of greens with garlic, lemon, and olive oil.

Trapp had never seen blue corn chips. Her mother had brought them from New York. She'd seen Gabby take a basket from her mother's hand and offer them around. Trapp crunched on one—it wasn't bad at all.

"Where's the seven-layer salad?" Maggie asked, whining. "You always make seven-layer salad." Iceberg lettuce layered with peas, bacon, cheddar cheese, mayonnaise, scallions, hard-boiled egg slices; it was true, her mother always brought one in a large casserole dish, to be tossed only after it sat for twenty-four hours in refrigeration.

155

"I don't know," their mother said thoughtfully. "I just didn't feel like putting one together yesterday. And Sam and your father and I got used to eating mixed green salads in New York—neither of you will believe how many different, exotic kinds of vegetables you can get at the specialty grocery stores. The variety is amazing."

Trapp's attention strayed. Grandma no longer seemed upset. She hustled in and out of the kitchen with all her usual energy, carrying over the rhubarb pies they had baked that morning and the blackberry cobblers put together right before dinner.

Dinner had already gone on for some time. The provisions gradually revived exhausted harvesters who had labored all day over Grandma's garden or those who had brought in the sweet corn for husking. Those "womenfolk," as Grandpa would say, had turned one of the outbuildings into an extra kitchen with portable burners and extension cords for canning and pickling and readied the crop for distribution.

That would continue into the next day, and maybe even the next. Trapp was still astonished that the work of two weeks could be condensed, with help, into a long weekend. Yet more skilled harvesters arrived in the afternoon, courtesy of Rakes—and his timely invocation of tribal ancestors. They had never had so many people gathered in one place before, and maybe never would again.

From her summer on the farm, Trapp was in good shape. But her shoulder ached from the bulk of vanilla ice cream—also part of Grandma's dessert plan—that she had been churning out since her parents had arrived, now stored and solid in the cellar deep freeze.

Rakes joined Trapp as she was about to bite into her third helping of pork. "Cleaver's already in the barn," he told her.

"I'm ready," she answered through a mouthful of hot meat. She was stuffed and ready for action. "Maggie, when it's time for dessert, run down to the cellar for ice cream. Sam, you help," she said to her brother, sitting next to her at the long table.

"Who made you queen?" he asked roughly. Then he became agreeable. "Should we bring all the ice cream up at once?"

"Yes," she said. "Grandpa has a cooler next to him—that will keep it frozen, I hope. And, Sam . . ." she added, looking at him.

"Yeah?" he asked.

"Could you stoke the fire in the pit with some wood? They don't need it anymore for cooking. Wood's out back."

"Sure," Sam repeated hesitantly. "But why?"

Trapp didn't answer.

"Ready?" Rakes said.

"Where're you going?" Maggie asked. "I want to come along."

"In a while," Trapp said, feeling quivery. She got to her feet and slipped down the path to the barn. She was still excited to be included. Rakes and Cleaver had planned this night.

The moon had risen into view behind the fields of dent

corn when Trapp and Cleaver emerged from the barn, and was hanging just above the horizon like a large orange spotlight. "Perfect," she breathed out through her costume.

"Yup," said Cleaver. "We couldn't have asked for a better set design."

They both disappeared into the high stalks and made their way to the appointed meeting place with Rakes. Twenty feet ahead were the band of barbecuers on the lawn, and beyond that, the Hatfield home. A white cloud of smoke streamed into the sky; Sam had indeed built up the fire.

The laughter and jostling of relatives finishing up their desserts were overrun by the sweet lowing of a flute-like instrument. The sound made Trapp ache, made her wonder if Rakes hurt as he played. She and Cleaver stood ready as the notes floated over the stalks of corn, wafting toward the fire, silencing the sounds of forks and spoons that scraped up the last berries and ice cream from stoneware plates. A hush crept over the crowd, winding through conversations like a vine.

Trapp shook slightly as Rakes sent each long tone out, his face dappled bronze as the firelight edged through the tall stalks of corn. The notes filled her with an odd anticipation that had started in her feet and traveled clear up her spine. Its slow-paced melody was haunting, but welcoming, too, as if it carried a young girl's message of hope and reassurance—that she was connected, that her past secrets and future life were with her in the fields, and that her voyage, anywhere in the world, would never be a lonely one.

The last note echoed over the still crowd, and Rakes put the flute down, then picked up the costume that had rested next to him on the ground.

Trapp and Cleaver had remained bent over at the waists, keeping their artificially tall forms out of view.

The three of them slowly stood up straight and began to make careful progress toward the fire.

Trapp was aching to know just what the crowd of cobbler eaters had seen.

The moon lightened to pale ivory as the sky deepened around them, and gave Rakes's sacred ground in the cornpatch an eerie blue cast. Then, just as the people by the fire began to shift in their seats, one, two, three pumpkin-sized heads appeared, silhouetted against the moon as they spiraled up high, higher, spinning and growing taller than any man or woman. Blank faces stared out above too-skinny shoulders and limp arms that dangled on either side of the outlines like ribbons from a maypole.

As the scarecrow-like figures moved toward the crowd, three pairs of arms sprang up, each making a V on either side of the body, long, unearthly arms with hands made of half-shucked ears of corn. The figures bobbed and danced through cornstalks, tall as ladders, toward Grandpa and Grandma Hatfield, dipped toward Gabby and Don, spun past Aunt Lily, Blissful Anne and Joy, and their father, passed over dozens of other relatives, paused by Trapp's mother, father, Maggie, and Sam, then lined up and began to skate around the outskirts of the fire. The bottoms of the scarecrows were covered in jeans and tucked into black boots, stomping around the flames and packing the dirt around the pit into a compact, still-warm surface.

"That's Cleaver," Maggie cried, then, in a weaker voice, added, "I think."

"Aw, it's just Trapp," Sam said ferociously, then asked, "Isn't it?"

Faster and faster the three figures spun around the fire, until Joy and Blissful Anne, unable to sit still, joined the circle. Other children were quick to imitate them—even fearful Maggie, even skeptical Sam. Some of the adults stepped in, too, while Grandpa, contentment on his face, watched the spectacle next to Grandma.

"We'd better join the harvest dance," he said quietly. Trapp, mid-spin as she passed him, barely made out his words. She glimpsed Grandma press her hand down on his shoulder as he motioned to get up. "I've known Rakes doing this sorta powwow since I was a boy. Never seen a livelier crowd," he said. Grandma patted his shoulder, shaking her head with a smile. "We should get the family out here every year."

Despite the frenzy, Trapp realized that Grandpa didn't mean just Rakes but Rakes's father, and his father's father, too. Now it was all a hodgepodge to her—physically and mentally. Maybe she had just eaten too quickly before the ceremony. Maybe Grandpa had.

Then it came to her, clearly. The answer. Not about Rakes. Not about moving.

That, no, she wouldn't tell. Trapp knew now that no one else would ever see the hidden initials and know their meaning—she had only found them by—by random, a series of events that seemed too unbelievable to be real. Was it *really* by chance, or did her heart lead her to it?

Her family, the Hatfields, the Stuttgards—they were all related, and they all came from here, and no one really needed to know exactly how, or why, or what had come before.

Buoyantly, she gripped the broomstick harder that held the head—a paper bag decorated with a face and, for hair, dried tassels that Cleaver had taken off the stalk right after they had turned from green to reddish brown to indicate the corn was pollinated—and body of the scarecrow well over her head. With all her strength, Trapp pushed the other stick that made the hands flap madly up and down, and spun, and spun, and spun until the fire died down and she, at Rakes's barely discernible bow, was allowed to flee back into the corn with him and Cleaver and fall over breathlessly into the soil, laughing her heart out.

In which, after a
long spell of conversations,
introspections, and a few broken
boards, a way is found to escape to
New York, gracefully

C ome on, honey," Trapp's mother called from the
backseat of the airport limousine they had hired.
"We have to make our flight." Trapp was sad to
see their Lincoln left behind—perhaps for good. Her father had mentioned something about a new Mercedes-
Benz, but she wasn't impressed.

Trapp had been sitting contentedly by Grandpa's knee
as he sat in the rocking chair. She felt settled in, and not
at all someone who was about to travel farther than she
ever cared to. She had told the Hatfields goodbye, but
couldn't make herself look at their faces too closely.

Trapp's father approached and took her by the hand,
then strolled with her through the yard.

"I'm fine, Dad. Really," Trapp said.

"It's not you I'm worried about. It's those who're left

behind," her father said. "We have to have a long talk, later, you and I. There are some things we need to sort out. As soon as we're all in New York."

He walked toward Gabby, who had been sitting at the edge of the porch, leaning against the wall, holding a coffee cup. He smiled at her, and she smiled back at both of them, sipping from her cup. "She's been up before the roosters," Grandpa had said.

"God willing, we're going to see quite a lot of her in New York," her father said. "She'll be quite nearby; we're practically on top of her. Your mother and I are just getting to know her, and she seems to be very fond of *you*. She did mention something about you and her meadow —I guess I don't know why I'm telling you all this now."

"Dad?" Trapp interrupted, stopping. "Did we buy Gabby's house from her or inherit it?"

"A little bit of both, you could say," her father answered. "She sold it to us for a song—muttered something about keeping it in the family."

"Is she the reason we're moving to New York?" Trapp asked.

"Good God, no," he hastily said. "She's one of many reasons, Trapp. And she's one great, wonderful person. I promise you'll find that out for yourself one day."

"Perhaps I already have," Trapp admitted.

Several goodbyes followed, and then, at the limousine, Trapp waved to her great-grandparents one last time. She looked for Cleaver, but he had disappeared. She hadn't told *him* goodbye—not properly.

163

"I'll be right back," she told her mother. She skipped over to the barn, knowing he was inside, that he couldn't be anywhere else.

"I can't believe I've had an attack of shyness in my old age," Cleaver said as she entered the barn, and before she had even spoken. He was perched on the desk, the dear old desk, with the initials. Her grandpa had noticed, he told her, that the center drawer wasn't working, and had told the Salvation Army movers to leave it there for him to fix—he probably said that every year. In eleven months or so, they would come for it again. It sat, alone, in the middle of the barn. She estimated that Cleaver, a wry smile on his face, was just about on top of the "secret."

Trapp grinned and shook her head. She walked right up and sat down next to him on the desk.

"You're as good as gone," he finally said. A long silence followed. "You're really ready."

"Nope," Trapp said. "I'm just really moving on, I guess. I'll never be really ready."

"Well," he said, "Harriet and Jim hope you'll come back soon."

"And who are Harriet and Jim?" she asked.

"Owners of the Alpine Inn. Exit 4," he replied. He tossed the baseball high into the air and caught it easily.

"And just how," she heard herself asking, "do you know that Harriet and Jim want me to come back soon?"

"You'll see on your way out of town," Cleveland answered. "There's a big new sign with a Campbell's corn chowder advertisement, and then the billboard for the Al-

pine Inn. 'Even if you're just stopping and looking, don't leave without trying Harriet's home cooking.'"

Trapp guffawed, and Cleveland, instead of waiting for his most recent toss to fall into his mitt, took a bow, still sitting, and let the ball roll away in the straw. Trapp leaned over to pick it up, rubbed it on her shirt as if polishing an apple, and handed it back. She felt awkward. Until she saw his eyes, unnaturally lit up like Grandpa Hatfield's. He averted his eyes, staring down at his mitt.

Staring down, thinking.

Trapp did the only thing she could think of, the one act that drew her toward him.

It made sense.

She found herself cuffing him on the shoulder with her mitt.

It worked. Something worked.

He looked at her from the corner of his eye, then cuffed her right back. He looked back at his mitt, and then, almost imperceptibly, brushed his hand against hers, as if to grasp it. She felt his touch, felt his fingers start to close around her hand, and wondered, fleetingly, what it would be like if she just stayed motionless until he had a hold on her.

The honk of the limousine drove the thought from her mind, and she leaped up, pulling away. And faster than her speedball pitch, she kissed Cleaver, on the forehead, and ran from him without looking back. "Corn can travel!" he called out. "I read it somewhere!"

Such funny parting words, and then she was opening the car door.

Maggie and Sam were already in the backseat, ready to begin their long-awaited exodus to New York. Arranging her knees together inside the car, Trapp closed the door behind her. She refused to look at the barn—unable to make herself believe that she was really leaving all of it, all of them, behind.

Her father sat in the front seat, and Sam and Maggie began to chatter at her at once. Then the engine died, and everyone stopped talking as quickly as they had begun.

In the silence, Trapp saw the farmhouse, and the land around it, and the sky that enclosed it all.

In the silence, she heard a distant thud-slap as Cleveland popped the ball off the side of the barn and caught it in his mitt.

And in the silence, a split second before the car roared back to life and they drove down the road, Trapp heard a sound—an almost familiar noise. First there was the crack of solid barn wood, and then a revelatory whoop of joy so real—so heartfelt—that Trapp knew its echo would stay with her all the way to their newly adopted home in the big city.